PRAISE FOR *SUN DON'T SHINE*

"Beautiful, raw, and achingly honest, *Sun Don't Shine* illuminates the precarious existence and morally complex choices of sixteen-year-old Reece, her volatile father, and those living on the dark fringes of the Sunshine state."

—Jennifer Salvato Doktorski, author of *August and Everything After*

SUN DON'T SHINE

Crissa-Jean Chappell

Fitzroy Books

Published by Fitzroy Books
An imprint of
Regal House Publishing, LLC
Raleigh, NC 27605
All rights reserved

https://fitzroybooks.com
Printed in the United States of America

ISBN -13 (paperback): 9781646034307
ISBN -13 (epub): 9781646034314
Library of Congress Control Number: 2023934875

Cover images and design by © C. B. Royal

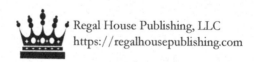

Regal House Publishing, LLC
https://regalhousepublishing.com

The following is a work of fiction created by the author. All names, individuals, characters, places, items, brands, events, etc. were either the product of the author or were used fictitiously. Any name, place, event, person, brand, or item, current or past, is entirely coincidental.

Printed in the United States of America

for Tom, Cathy, Tim and Caren

1

When somebody moves out, they always leave stuff behind. If I'm lucky, it was there all along, waiting for me to find it.

Today I'm not so lucky.

Dad stands guard as I swing my leg over the dumpster.

"Hustle up, Reece," he says, glancing across the parking lot. "You hear me?"

"I'm hustling," I mutter.

Traffic pounds the highway. All those cars are going where I can't go—away from here. Right now "here" is the Surfside, which might be the dumbest name ever. You won't find much surf in Miami.

The motel's neon sign says, SWIMMING POOL, AIR CONDITIONING, ASK ABOUT OUR WEEKLY RATES. The so-called pool is clogged with dead leaves. Most of the time it's empty. Unless it rains.

"Thanks, dumpster gods," I whisper, scooping a crumpled dollar out of a jeans pocket. I'm real good at finding money. No joke. I keep my head down everywhere I go, scanning the sidewalk for loose pennies. Money twitches like a living thing. It moves a certain way. Catches my eye with its quiet breathing.

Dad gives the signal, whistling through his teeth. Somebody's coming. I hunch down a little lower. The dumpster smells so freaking gross. As I tug the collar of my T-shirt over my nose, trying not to inhale the hot stink of rotten bananas, I hear Booth screaming his head off.

"I better not catch you stealing out of the trash."

Booth is the freak in charge of this motel. He always wears a leather jacket bristling with patches, even if it's a hundred degrees outside. "His light don't reach the top floor," Dad likes to say, tapping his forehead.

"What the hell are you doing out here?" Booth yells.

"Just out for a walk," Dad tells him.

"Yeah? Then start walking. You're behind rent," he says. "I could have you out tomorrow."

"I'm working on it."

"Work a little harder." Booth slams his fist against the dumpster and I flinch. It really sucks that he's going off on Dad. Still, I hold my breath. If he catches me stealing junk, I'm in big trouble.

After what seems like forever, Dad whistles again.

Back to work.

My legs are zombie-numb, squashed under a mound of garbage bags. Feels like clothes, judging by the lumpy shapes. I punch my fingers through the sun-baked plastic, rip open a bag, and start digging.

It's crazy, the stuff people throw away. I dig out a paperback and flip through the wrinkled pages. It's one of those cheesy romance books with a half-naked dude on the cover. Doesn't matter what it's about. I'll pretty much read anything. Who throws a book in the trash? Brain-dead idiots. That's who.

The bag is full of kiddie stuff. A friendship bracelet, the kind you wear until it rots off. Pink sneakers and a denim jacket so small, I could probably sew it into a skirt. Too bad I'm not a fan of sewing. Or skirts.

Dad could probably sell most of this crap online. I'll let him sort through this mess once we're back in our motel room. I launch the Hefty bag over the edge of the dumpster with a thunk. It's weird that somebody tossed out all those baby clothes. They must've been hauling ass.

I didn't know their names, but I remember the little girl and her dad. At least, I think he was her dad. Could've been her mom's boyfriend or whatever. He used to sit on a milk crate in the parking lot and watch his kid zigzag between the cars. She'd scoop up bottle caps in her fist and carry them back like a prize.

"Wow, sweetie. That's so beautiful," he'd say, as if that bottle cap was worth a million dollars. She'd smile and go running off to find more. When she wasn't looking, he'd toss them in the bushes.

"Hustle," Dad shouts.

I pull myself out of the dumpster. My legs are blotchy with scrapes and bruises. It feels like I'll never be clean again. I glance across the parking lot. "Is he gone?"

"Yeah, Booth's long gone. That was a close one." Dad slings a garbage bag over his shoulder like a crackhead Santa. "Now let's get out of here."

As we carry our loot back to the motel, I peer into the bushes. Sure enough, the bottle caps are scattered in the dirt. Their sharp edges glint in the sun, handfuls of silver and gold so bright, I can't see the rust.

After my triumph over the dumpster gods, we plunk our quarters in a sock, then walk a couple blocks to Wendy's. It's not far from the motel, but walking anywhere in Miami is a mission. We pass the botanica with the dried scorpions and coyote skulls grinning in the front window. There's a dude with no shirt pushing a shopping cart loaded with mangoes down the sidewalk. He probably stole that fruit from somebody's backyard.

By the time we get to Wendy's, the place is packed. It's not even lunchtime yet and the tables are filled with old ladies with gold hoop earrings and head-to-toe Spandex. They stare big time as me and Dad push through the door.

"My treat," he says, even though I did all the work. He dumps the sock on the counter. I really wish he'd toss that piece of crap.

I squint at the menu. All my teachers think I need glasses, but that's just another thing I can't afford.

Dad orders vanilla Frosties for both of us. "The biggest size you got."

"Want extra whip on that?" asks the girl behind the cash register. She's got eyebrows so pale, they're almost see-through.

"No thanks," I say, reaching for my shake. I refuse to say

"Frosty." It's so annoying when you have to order something with a stupid name.

He snatches the cup out of my hand. "What's wrong with you? Get your money's worth." He shoves it across the counter. "She wants sprinkles," he says like I'm not even standing there. "Rainbow sprinkles. That's her favorite."

I wince. "Come on, Dad. I'm sixteen. Not two."

"Everybody wants sprinkles."

"Well, I don't, okay?"

The cashier pushes back her hair and sighs. "Frosties don't come with sprinkles."

"They do now," he says, crossing his arms.

"I'm sorry, sir, but I can't break the rules."

"Dad, it's no big deal," I tell him. "Seriously. I don't want sprinkles."

"Yes, you do!" he hollers. The grey-haired lady in a booth near the window twists around and blinks. He probably blew out her hearing aid. Then he pushes that stupid sock at the cashier.

"I could throw in some Oreo crunchies, if you want," she says.

"Perfect." He nods. "You're cool with Oreos, aren't you, Reecey?"

I want to say no, but it's easier to give in.

"Yeah, I'm cool with Oreos."

"And fries," he adds. Because there's nothing better than french fries dipped in vanilla ice cream. That's one thing me and Dad can agree on.

We march out the door into the blazing sun. As we wait to cross the street, I punch the Walk button. Does it actually make the light change faster? Or does it give you the thrill of accomplishing something when you're just wasting time?

"That girl should be fired," Dad says, dunking a fry in my shake.

I suck down that vanilla sludge so fast, the space between my eyes burns. "She's just doing her job."

He pops the fry in his mouth. "But she's doing it wrong."

When we get back to our motel room, I dig through the garbage bags on the floor. It's like dumping out your trick-or-treat bag on Halloween. I'm looking for whatever Dad can sell on eBay. Stuffed bears filled with plastic beans. Tangled hoops of Christmas lights. You won't believe the crap we've sold online.

I scrape the price tag off a candle in a glass jar. For some reason, people go crazy over candles with names like Pumpkin Spice and Parisian Daydream (I'm not even sure what that smells like).

"Find any jewelry?" Dad asks.

I shake my head.

We're saving up for the Holy Trinity—first, last, and security. In other words, our own apartment.

Yeah, like that's going to happen.

Dad's got the junk sorted into piles: KEEP. EBAY. TOSS. He's even scrounged up a half-eaten bag of Gummi Bears. That stuff lasts forever. Trust me. If a nuclear bomb wiped out Planet Earth, the only things left would be Gummi Bears and radioactive cockroaches.

I sneak the bag of Gummies in my pocket. "So what happened to the people next door?"

Dad's messing with an ancient '80s boombox, trying to pry it open with a screwdriver. "What people?"

"Room 22. It's their stuff."

"Who?" He squints.

"Did that family get kicked out?"

"How the hell should I know?" Dad smacks the boombox and a million batteries clatter across the floor.

When Dad's on the verge of a rage fest, it's a good idea to chill and leave him alone. His moods change so fast, I can't keep up. Just like that, he'll be goofing around again and it's like I'm stuck in a TV show with a never-ending laugh track. And I can't change the channel.

I'll be doing homework and Dad's like, "Check this out." I feel bad if I try to ignore him. *Try* is the key word. You can't ignore somebody if you're trapped inside the same motel room.

"Reecey-Piece," he says. "Look."

Will he ever stop calling me that?

I scoot next to him on the bed (that's my "homework desk" and our dining room table) and check out the Exciting Thing my dad thinks is hysterical. Usually it's rich people in magazines. In other words, people I don't care about.

"What's she trying to be?" he says, flipping through *Us Week-ly*'s "Stars—They're Just Like Us!"

"She's a person. You know. Two arms, two legs."

"She's a bomb-ass singer, though," he says like they're on a first name basis.

"Dad, please don't say bomb-ass."

Sometimes I forget that Dad's actually kind of young. When we go for Grand Slams at Denny's, the waitress thinks I'm his little sister. Still, I wish he'd chop off that stupid ponytail. I mean, come on. Dad sticks out his middle finger. "I can say whatever I want. I'm a grown-ass man."

That's what he thinks.

"Look at this, Reecey," he says, snapping pages. "She's got a pet pig. And they sleep together. I hope that pig wears a diaper." He snorts a laugh and I can't help it. I laugh too. Yeah, my dad's super annoying most of the time, but he's also a lot of fun.

"Okay," I tell him. "Can you give me some space? I really need to work on my Greek mythology paper."

"So work on it."

"But I need space."

"You've got plenty of space."

Dad really doesn't get it.

I need space away from him.

I kick a Hefty Sak off the bed. The bag flops over, spilling out more baby clothes and an awesome pair of Converse high tops. I grab them by the laces, dangling like a fish on a hook. "Oh my god. Sweet."

Dad frowns. "Put that back. It goes in the sell pile."

"Why?"

"Those shoes are worth good money."

"But my sneakers are falling apart."

"Don't be so dramatic." He shakes his fist.

Now who's being dramatic?

I cram my foot into that sneaker like I'm some kind of motel Cinderella. To my surprise, it fits perfectly. Who knew?

Dad yanks the sneaker off so fast, I slam backward against the wall. A battery rolls across the floor, but I don't dare pick it up.

"You have enough shoes," he says, which isn't true. I've got a couple of no-name combat boots and a knock-off pair of TOMS. That's it. I had to Super-glue the rubber soles back together, they're so damn cheap.

I rub the sting out of my eyes. "Shut up, Dad."

He spins around. "Don't give me that smart mouth," he says like I'm the one who's crazy. "Unbelievable." Dad's favorite thing to say when he's pissed. "Do you have any clue how hard I work?" he says, revving full speed into Rage Mode. "I break my goddamn back so we can have nice things. You know that?"

Yeah, I know, Dad. You work real hard. That's what you tell me. Every single day. And for the record, we never have "nice things."

Last summer we were sleeping in our van in Orlando. Dad scored a part-time job at Target. Guest services. That's just a fancy name for "dude who greets people at the door." Still, the money wasn't enough.

At night we steered the van to a rest stop near Disney World. That was home. I brushed my teeth over the bathroom sink. Scraped food out of the garbage. Half-moons of burger meat. That was dinner. When the sun dribbled away, I'd curl up in the backseat and listen to the fireworks going off—*boom, crackle, boom*. I never actually saw the rockets sizzle across the sky. A couple months later, me and Dad packed up all our stuff and drove south to Miami.

There's a reason we never stay in one place long. A reason we don't talk about. I offered to help out. Get a job waiting tables or something. Dad said no. It's too risky.

"We can't take a chance like that, needle legs," he told me. "I'm the only one you've got in this world."

Dad always calls me needle legs, even though I'm not a skinny little kid anymore. If he doesn't find a job soon, I'm going to be a lot skinnier. Right now he's "between gigs," which basically means we're homeless. He says it's just a temporary thing, but I'm not buying it.

"Come on," he says, easing next to me on the bed. All rage gone. "The shit hasn't hit the fan yet, okay? Smile. You're so much prettier when you smile."

Who says I have to be pretty? A sickly tang hangs over the motel room, reminding me of burnt plastic. The zombies must be free-basing under the stairs. Booth won't do jack about it. I bet he's a zombie too. Every night, he stumbles into the parking lot and starts hosing down his truck, the lime-green Ford with the American flag peeling across the back window. At least he's putting his cracked-out energy to good use.

I get up and squint through the dusty blinds. I've memorized every stain in the cheap drywall, the fluorescent lights blurred with dead moths. I used to pretend those bugs were fairies, but I'm too old to believe in shit like that.

"Why did we have to move here?"

It's not the first time I've asked.

Dad snaps the blinds shut. "Give it time. We'll be out of this dump by Christmas."

We'll be kicked out if we don't pay rent.

"Things are going to get better," he says, chucking that sweet pair of Converse into the eBay box. "I promise."

Dad's promises are worth less than those beat-up old sneakers. I can't stand being trapped in this room. There's never enough space to breathe. I grab my tote bag and inch toward the door.

"Where do you think you're going?" he says.

"Where else? The oasis." That's what we call the gas station across the street.

"And do what? Smoke?"

"Who cares? You smoke all the time. I bet your lungs are all shriveled up."

"That's exactly why you should stop. Uncle Frank got cancer. They found a lump in his larynx."

"His what?"

"Right here." Dad jabs his throat.

"Well, I never met him."

Dad barges in front of the door, blocking my way. "You going out dressed like that?"

I glance down at my cut-offs. "What's wrong with shorts?"

"Everything's hanging out," he says, looking away.

When Dad says "everything," he means my butt. It's not like I can magically shrink it back to G-rated proportions.

"But it's, like, ninety degrees outside."

"Did you hear what I said?"

Yeah, I heard.

I go into the bathroom and pull on my jeans. When I come out, Dad's back to messing with that ancient boombox.

"Much better," he says, barely glancing at me.

"Can I go now?"

"Don't take too long. Remember the rules, okay?"

Rule Number One: don't talk to strangers.

When I was a little kid, I wasn't allowed to go outside by myself. Somebody might recognize me. Then it's game over.

"Do me a favor," Dad says. "Get some new batteries while you're running around. I want to see if this thing still works."

"We're out of cash," I mumble, hoping this will get him off my back.

"So? Just do your thing."

My thing is stealing. It's what I'm good at.

Sometimes I wish it wasn't.

"Let's make a deal," he says. The magic words. "You help me out and I'll fry up some eggs and beans for dinner."

Just thinking about Dad's greasy black beans and rice makes my stomach burn. He's an amazing cook. No joke. We don't even have a fridge. All it takes is a power outlet. He always keeps a giant bag of yellow rice in a Keebler cracker tin. As long as we've got rice, we're good to go.

One time, me and Dad were dumpster diving behind Whole Foods on Biscayne Boulevard. A cop told us to leave and I was like, "We aren't stealing anything." Dad tore into a moldy hot dog bun and shoved it in his mouth.

"Same thing as blue cheese," he said, chewing. "Builds your immune system. That's how penicillin was discovered."

I draw the line at moldy hot dog buns, but here's the deal. Tons of perfectly decent food gets thrown out every day. And I'm telling you, it's still good. If there's a bruise on that organic banana, it's not going to kill you, I swear. When something's less than perfect, the store throws it out. Nobody's going to pay for it. That's what they think.

Of course, I wasn't actually paying.

It's been a long time since Dad cooked anything. Not that there's much to cook. He'll plug in the electric skillet and put me to work, chopping up peppers until the tears splat down my neck. When I was little, we used to blast Celia Cruz on the radio. Me and Dad would salsa dance with my feet balanced on his toes.

We never dance anymore.

Dad looks at me. "Can you do this?"

Yeah, I can totally do this.

But I don't want to.

"Okay. Fine."

Maybe now he'll leave me alone.

"Hold on." He scoops up something off the floor. My "pirate scarf."

I flinch. "Do I really have to wear that thing?"

"You know the rules." He tosses it at me.

"But I'm only going across the street."

"Now."

I tie the bandana across my forehead, pushing it down low. "Good girl," he says as I open the door. "And, needle legs…" "Yeah?" I turn around. "Keep your eyes wide open." "Whatever." I slam the door. The breezeway is strangely quiet. Nobody's out here except a little mousey-haired girl crouched on the steps outside Room 22. She throws her Barbie into the air and catches it over and over again. I can't tell if she's trying to murder that doll or teaching it to fly. I smile at her. "Moving in?" She doesn't smile back. "Here." I reach inside my bag and take out the bag of Gummies.

Mouse still doesn't move. It's like she's stuck on pause. Or maybe she's hypnotized by all the metal in my face. Last summer, I pierced my lip with a safety pin—snakebites, one on both sides—but the holes got infected and closed up. Thanks to the magic of YouTube, I finally got it right (you have to sterilize the needle with a match).

The piercing was Dad's idea. Same for my hair. We bleached my split ends for the full ombré effect. That's a fancy word that means "more than one color." Dad says it helps me blend in. That's one of his rules. Trust me. He's got a million.

"Everybody's wearing their hair like that," he told me.

I shrugged. "You're not."

At first, I was really into the bleach. It made me feel very Mother of Dragons. Then Ashleigh Coleman, this annoying girl in homeroom, did the same thing to her hair. Now half the school's gone ombré. It's really stupid, the way people copy each other all the time. If a magazine told them to wear coffee filters on their heads, they would do it.

Another thing that helps me blend in. I'm small, which means I could pass for a middle schooler. And don't say "fun-sized." Because there's nothing fun about scoring combat boots from the kiddie shelf at Goodwill.

I drop the bag of Gummies on the steps and head downstairs. On Saturdays, the old dudes play dominoes in the parking lot under the fluorescent lights. Dad says they're playing another game too—bolita—a secret underground version of the Florida Lotto. They scribble numbers on scraps of paper and pass them to the guy at the bodega on the corner.

"The game's rigged," Dad told me.

"Then why do they keep playing?"

He shrugged. "Because one day, they might get lucky."

When I glance back, the candy's gone.

So is the girl.

Sky rats.

That's what Dad calls the kids who drift in and out of this motel. He says me and him are different. We don't stick around long. Still, I can't help wondering what happened to the family in Room 22. Maybe they finally moved into a real house. At least, that's what I hope.

As I wait to cross the street, I watch a pigeon flutter and swoop above the motel's neon sign. When I was little, Dad used to say they turned into rats at night.

He never told me what people turn into.

2

The oasis is a quick walk from the motel, which is kind of ironic because our gas tank's always empty. Every weekend, the same boys rattle their skateboards across the cracked cement. Don't they have better things to do? Who knows. Maybe they're getting high off the fumes.

Now that Dad's gone, I tug off my bandana. I'm sick of wearing it all the time, and besides, I'm sweating like a mofo. I shove it in my tote bag and dig around for my trusty Zippo. I'm not big into smoking, but it gives me something to do. As I spark up a menthol, one of the boys skates over to me.

"Hey, can I see your lighter?" he calls out. Skinny kid with a serious tan. Here's the deal. When somebody asks to "see" whatever's in your hands, it's pretty obvious you're never going to see it again.

I keep walking.

He steps on the board and it pops up into his hand. "I said lighter."

"I said no."

"You didn't actually say it."

"I'm saying it now."

He grins. "So you like bats?"

I glance down at the cartoon on my tote bag—a vampire bat caught in mid-flap. ALL HAIL KALE says the bubble floating above its toothy grin. I stole this bag from the dumpster behind Whole Foods on Biscayne Boulevard. I don't even know what kale is. Some kind of rich people lettuce.

"I saw a bat once," he tells me. "They're like mice. Only they fly."

Okay. This boy is super random. Maybe this is his weird way of flirting. What do I know about boys? Zero. That's what. He's

bouncing on his toes and staring at me the whole time. Why is
he staring? I'll give you the reason.

It's called my face.

The stain above my left eyebrow is the color of those soy
sauce packets you get with Chinese take-out. From a distance,
it's the shape of a luna moth's wing. Up close, it's more like a
scab. It's always been there and it's never going away.

This is why I have to wear that stupid bandana. My pirate
scarf, Dad calls it. I'm not allowed to take it off. I even wear it
to bed. You'd think I'd be used to it by now, but I'll never get
used to all the stupid questions.

What's wrong with your face?

Did somebody hit you?

Does it hurt?

In kindergarten nobody wanted to sit next to me. They
thought my Stain was contagious. Some kind of disease. A
flesh-eating bacteria. Or a bruise that wouldn't heal. Dad said
when I got older, it would fade away.

He lied.

When I was little, my Stain was easier to hide. My luna moth
wings hadn't spread yet. Dad tried everything to make it go
away. Lemon juice. Wart cream. One time, he held me down
and burned my forehead with a match. A scar would look better. That's what he told me. The skin crusted over like dried
paint. Underneath the scab, my Stain bloomed in the same spot,
as if starting all over again.

I shouldn't have ditched my bandana. Big mistake. This boy
is way too curious about me. And he's wasting my time. If I
don't get back to the motel soon, Dad's going to kill me.

I start walking toward the oasis.

"Peace out," I tell Skinny.

"Wait," he says. "Where are you going?"

Where does he think I'm going?

I push open the door and head inside. This place has that
familiar stench of microwave burritos and Pine Sol. The con-
venience store's in full Halloween mode, even though it's only

September. A string of Christmas lights droops across the wall, the tiny bulbs shaped like jack-o'-lanterns. Wow. They've got all the holidays covered.

As I march down the aisles, the bald guy behind the counter looks up. He frowns, as if I'm messing with his Zen, and crumples up his newspaper. I bet he's got a porno hidden inside it.

"Need any help?" he asks.

He's not really asking.

"I'm good. Thanks." I grab a stick of beef jerky and pretend to study the label. It was easier when I was little. Stealing, I mean. Nobody expects a little girl to walk out of a gas station with a can of Bud Light tucked under her skirt.

I drift past a rack of keychains: I LOVE THE SUNSHINE STATE! A tray of hot dogs sweating under glass. Frozen slush the color of antifreeze. Shelves loaded with Extra-Energy vitamins in tiny plastic bags. I keep my eyes wide open. That's what Dad taught me, the night we ran away.

After searching all over the damn store, I spot the batteries near the cash register. A prime location, in case anyone tries to sneak out without paying. I slide the package off the hook. Then I reach inside my bag and take out my phone. I flip it open and stare at the screen like I'm reading a Very Important message. I do the count inside my head. One Mississippi. Two Mississippi. Then I walk outside, nice and slow.

"You forgot something."

Skinny again. He's actually waiting for me in the parking lot. He leans in close like we're sharing a secret.

"About that lighter," he whispers.

"Fine." Let him have the damn thing.

"Thanks," he says, as if I'm doing him a favor.

I stare at the giant freaking cross on his T-shirt. LIFE-GUARD it says, in case anyone doubts his life-saving abilities. He doesn't even spark up a cigarette. He's just messing with my Zippo. He tips it against his fist.

I roll my eyes. "Are you going to set yourself on fire now?"

"Nah. I'm saving that for later." He spreads out his fingers, clicks the lighter, and a flame bursts across his palm. Okay. That was kind of amazing, but if he thinks I'm going to start clapping, he better guess again.

"What the hell did you do to my Zippo?"

"I made it better. Now it's a super lighter."

"Is that supposed to impress me?"

He blinks. "Did it?"

"Maybe," I say, tapping out a cigarette.

He holds up the super lighter and almost burns my face off. "I always see you at that skanky motel," he says, jerking his head at the Surfside across the street. "Are you on some kind of permanent vacation?"

Vacation. Right. Because living in a motel is like Disney World. It freaks me out, the fact that he's noticed me. Boys are dangerous. That's what Dad drilled into my head. And if this boy noticed me, it means other people could've noticed too.

"No, I just hang out in the parking lot and smoke crack." My pathetic attempt at changing the subject. "So what's the deal? You're fireproof or something?"

"Working on it," he says. "I'm Shawn, by the way."

Shawn doesn't exactly fit my definition of a lifeguard. His arms are lean and sunburned, but not in a hanging-at-the-beach sort of way.

"You go to Bird Dick?" Shawn asks.

I bust out a giggle. My school's named after this dead guy, Admiral Richard Byrd. He flew to the North Pole a million years ago. I guess that's kind of a big deal. Maybe the school-naming people forgot that we live in South Florida.

"Yeah, I just started this year," I tell Lifeguard Shawn. "I'm a sophomore, but my dad makes me take AP everything."

"Me too," Shawn says. "I mean, I'm a sophomore too." He coughs like he's suddenly coming down with black lung or scurvy, one of those old-school pirate diseases. "Mystery solved."

"What mystery?"

"The reason why I've never seen you at school before."

"Well, now you've seen me."

Shawn stands there, grinning. His front teeth are perfectly straight and crossed by a slim metal wire. It seems like everybody's getting their braces off lately. I hope someday I can pay for stuff like that.

"So you think it's true?" he asks.

I take the bait.

"Maybe it's true," I say, blowing out smoke. "If I had a clue what you're talking about."

"Did Admiral Byrd, our school's great namesake, discover a secret hole in the center of the earth?"

This boy is definitely a weirdo.

"How big was the hole?" As soon as it pops out of my mouth, I wince. "Sorry. That sounded kind of perverted."

"No worries. That was only PG on the pervert scale. So the earth's supposed to be hollow, right? Admiral Byrd wrote about it in his diary. He saw all kinds of weird shit. Wooly mammoths and stuff."

"Sounds like a good place to hide a wooly mammoth."

Shawn laughs. "Who says they're hiding?"

It's been so long since I had a random conversation with somebody my age. Not to mention, this boy is kind of cute. But I really need to get back to the motel.

He looks over his shoulder. "Here comes the gas station mafia."

At first I think he means his friends, but the parking lot's empty. His crew must've took off. So much for brotherhood. Then I notice the old dude from the oasis waddling toward us.

"This ain't no playground," he says, waving like we're only capable of understanding hand signals. Obviously he hates his life. "Get out. Or I'm calling the cops."

I shiver.

Rule Number Two: keep away from cops.

Dad's told me a million times. The police aren't your "friend." They don't hang around the motel keeping us safe. They're only out for themselves. And if they find us, you can bet my dad's going to jail.

"Hear what I said? Move." The old dude is still trying to shoo us away. He doesn't care if we get flattened by a car. He's just another human with robot parts, functioning on autopilot.

Shawn tucks his skateboard under his arm. "God, you'd think we were criminals or something."

"Yeah, for real."

Is he onto me?

I flick my cigarette into a puddle where it floats with the dead leaves. Smoking makes me feel okay for a limited time, then I run out of cancer sticks and need to buy more. Like I said, it gives me something to do. Or else I start thinking too much. And when I think too much, I get freaking scared. And when I'm scared, my brain goes full speed into the darkness.

"Well, I really have to go," I tell him.

It's late. Or maybe it just feels late. Shawn follows me across the street, his arm swinging next to mine. It doesn't seem like he's in a hurry to leave. We walk past a Cadillac that's been rusting in the same spot so long, the windshield is plastered with tickets. The sky's getting dark, the clouds stacked like dinosaur bones.

When I was little, I wanted to be an archeologist. Dad said forget it. Girls don't run around "digging up dead things." That's what he thinks. I can't help wondering if there are any mammoths hiding somewhere on the earth. Or a planet that humans haven't messed up yet.

If everybody in Miami got wiped out by a killer comet, the city would sink back into a jungle a lot faster than you'd imagine. In a hundred years, we'd find oak trees sprouting through the gas stations. Nothing but wild dogs and flocks of parrots saying hello to nobody. I can't decide if that sounds really awesome or depressing.

Shawn stares at me so hard, my face heats up and I quickly look away. It's like he's eavesdropping on my brain. "You're so quiet."

"Is that bad?" I'm still thinking about the lonely parrots.

He shrugs. "What's your name again?"

"It's Reece."

Why is he asking so many questions?

As we get closer to the motel, I dig inside my Hail Kale bag and take out my phone. I'm not actually texting anybody. Just punching random buttons. Call it my invisible force field. Morse Code for *go away*. Dad gave me this cheap-ass phone for "emergencies." In other words, I'm not supposed to use it.

"Does your phone come with designer cracks in it?" Shawn asks. "Like those fake bullet holes that people stick on their trucks?"

"Wow. That's so funny, I forgot to laugh."

"But you did," he says.

And he's right.

My phone is blurred with cracks. I can barely read the crap I'm typing: *la la la*. I could take this piece of junk somewhere and get it fixed, but that costs too much. Whatever. Dad probably stole it.

I squint at the numbers on the screen.

Shit.

Dad's already sent a bunch of crazy texts:

TIME'S UP!!!!!

WHERE ARE YOU?

I bet he's already in the parking lot, looking for me. God, how could I be so stupid? I need to get back to the motel before he loses it.

"I really have to leave," I tell Shawn.

"What's the rush?"

"My dad's waiting for me. He's kind of freaking out." I shove the phone in my bag. I can't let anybody see it. If the motel people spot something they want, it's just a matter of time. They'll take it.

"So what are the batteries for?"

My face burns. Shawn probably thinks I stole those batteries just for fun. I don't know. How am I supposed to explain that Dad's selling crap on eBay because we can't pay rent?

I glance up at the breezeway on the second floor. Door 22

is flung wide open. Boxes everywhere. God, that was quick. No sign of human life. I don't even see Mouse with her suicidal Barbie.

What do I see?

Dad's smoking a cigarette on the stairs. A couple minutes ago, he was giving me the cancer speech. Uncle Frank's lumpy larynx. Whatever. I don't know shit about my family. That's the way he wants it. Who knows? Maybe everybody's dead. And if Dad catches me talking to a boy, I'll be dead too.

"I have to go," I tell Shawn.

Too late.

Dad's already marching down the steps. Even worse, he's in his "jogging pants." I'm sorry, but sweats don't count as pants. And my dad doesn't jog. He does push-ups on the floor and calls it "gym."

Shawn stares at him. "Is that your dad?"

Please God. Just kill me now.

"Yeah. How did you guess?"

"He kind of looks like you."

"For real?" I seriously hope he's joking.

"There's a certain resemblance," he says, twisting his mouth into a scowl.

"Do I really look that bad?"

"Not bad," he says. "Just mean."

So that's how I look.

Before I can say anything, Dad marches up to us. His face is splotchy with rage. This is going to be a completely new level of hell. Not that I believe in hell or the devil or all that boiling pit of fire stuff. It's pretty obvious I'm already living in it.

"If there's one thing I can't stand, it's liars," Dad says, as if anybody cares. "Do you hear me, Reece?"

Yeah, I heard.

Shawn drops his skateboard on the ground. "Catch you later," he says, rattling across the parking lot.

Coward.

Dad's screaming at full volume, making a big deal about

nothing, as usual. That's his special talent. "Thought you went across the street."

"I was just walking back," I mutter.

"That's not what it looks like."

"See?" I wave the pack of Double As in his face.

He grabs my arm. "Who's that boy I saw you talking to?"

"Just some boy. I don't know." I try to wiggle out of Dad's grip, but he's lost in the rage-zone, tuning me out.

"You absolutely cannot talk to boys. It's too dangerous," he says, yanking me toward the stairs. "Do I have to go over the rules again?"

The rules.

I'm so sick of Dad's rules.

Rule Number Three: don't let anyone get close.

It's not just boys I have to worry about. I never really had any friends. No besties. No Friday night slumber parties. Of course, when you're living in a motel, it's hard to make friends. At least, the kind who stick around.

"This is going to stop. Right now," Dad says as he drags me upstairs.

"But I didn't do anything."

In the breezeway, a lady with plastic curlers is keeping an eye on the fun. God, why doesn't she take a picture?

Dad yanks open the door to our room. "Get in."

I back away from the roach scooting up the wall. I swear, in all the fucked-up places we've lived, I've never seen bugs this huge. It's like the Miami roaches are on steroids. And that's not the worst part. If you get too close, they fly.

"Move," Dad says.

"I'm moving." I lift my combat boot and check out the sliver of glass sticking out of the flimsy rubber. There's so much broken stuff all over the place, it's kind of unavoidable.

"This is not going to happen again." Dad pushes me inside the room. "No more trips across the street."

He's got to be kidding.

"What? I can't go outside and take a walk?"

"You heard me."

"So what are you going to do? Chain me up?"

"The door's right there," he says, jerking his thumb. "Go ahead, if you feel like running away."

"You mean, like you ran away from Mom?"

He smacks me across the face.

I'm so stunned, it takes me a second to realize what's going on. White-hot pain zings across my cheek. I run straight for the bathroom and punch the lock. Only then do I let the tears burn.

"Reece?" Dad pounds on the door. "Open up."

Why? So you can beat the shit out of me?

"I'm not saying it again," he yells.

Then don't.

Dad jiggles the handle. He throws his weight against the door so hard, it shudders. It's only a matter of time before he busts through it. Believe me. Dad's real good at getting into places. I've seen him pick locks with a butter knife.

"Go away, Dad," I whisper. "Drop dead."

As soon as the thought pops up, I feel bad.

When I was little, I used to pray that me and Dad would die at the same time. I really couldn't deal with the idea of being alone. What if there's no such thing as heaven? No castle floating in the sky. No long lost dogs galloping across the clouds to lick your face. If that's true, I'll never know. Because I'll be worm food.

I must've done something good in my past life. Dad finally gives up. The TV clicks on—a low-pitched buzz that I sense more than hear. I'm shaking all over. Dad's never hit me before. Never.

On the shower rod, my sopping wet jeans are dangling like skins, dripping in 4/4 time. I wring them out in the sink. I'm aching to scrub off the dumpster dirt, but the water in this motel is always ice cold. My strategy? Wait until everybody goes to sleep late at night. Then I've got a halfway decent chance of lukewarm water.

I reach down and scratch the welts on my ankle. The motel's

crawling with bed bugs. When somebody moves out, they drag their mattresses to the street. Then somebody else drags it back inside—bugs and all. Between that and the flying roaches, it's an endless circle of doom.

I get in the shower and tug off my shorts, but leave my T-shirt on. That way it gets washed. And let's be real. I'm probably wearing it again tomorrow. I keep my flip-flops on too. Around here, there's no telling what you'll step on. Trust me. Broken glass is the least of my worries. I can't remember the last time I walked around barefoot.

Today sucked on so many levels. I've never seen Dad freak out like that before. He's been getting a lot worse lately. The rage fests, I mean. He won't let me have any space to myself. Who am I kidding? I've been stuck under his control ever since he took me away from Mom.

I don't know how much longer I can deal with this. Dad's mood swings. The constant moving from one shitty place to another. All I want to do is run away, but we've been running so long, there's no place left to hide.

Sometimes I think about going to the cops. I could just march up to the police station and say, "Hey, remember that little girl who disappeared ten years ago? Well, guess what? That's me!"

But then Dad would go to jail.

The shower's freezing cold. I cross my arms and shiver. I think about Shawn, his easygoing laugh. Will I see him tomorrow at school? Or will he pretend we never talked at all?

I let the water hammer my back.

I'd rather feel nothing than live in this skin.

3

A long time ago, I slept in my own bedroom. Not a dirty mattress on the floor. I didn't hear gunshots late at night. Rain drummed the roof and swayed the mango tree outside my window. It was good when it rained. Then I couldn't hear Mom and Dad fighting.

I used to have a lot of nice things. A jewelry box studded with seashells. A lacey white dress I wore to my first Communion. As soon as church ended, I climbed the mango tree in that dress. I never wanted to take it off.

On my bookshelf, the faint blue glow of my fish tank threw shadows on the wall. Dad picked out guppies for me. We named them after the planets in the sky. Mars. Venus. Pluto. Dad told me they wouldn't die as fast as goldfish.

I never got a chance to find out.

At night, my fish tank glowed like the star map in Miss Garcia's classroom. My guppies were tiny planets spinning around the sun. Mom and Dad slept in the room next to me. Except they didn't sleep. They yelled.

"Think I like breaking my back all day?" Dad shouted through the wall. "I didn't plan on this."

"Yeah?" Mom screamed back. "Well, I didn't plan on having kids."

I tugged the blanket over my head.

Something crashed against my bedroom wall. There was the teeth-clenching noise of shattered glass. Then silence.

Next thing I knew, Dad was squeezing my shoulder. Why didn't he turn on the light? I barely recognized his face floating in the darkness.

"Am I in trouble?" I whispered.

"No, sweetie. We're taking a little trip," he said, answering the question in my mind.

"Where are we going?"

Dad had promised if we saved up enough money, we'd go to Disney World and ride the spinning tea cups with Princess Jasmine. So far, it hadn't happened.

"Away," he said.

I couldn't picture away.

"Away where?"

For a minute, he stayed quiet. "We're going camping."

I watched the tiny shapes hover in the tank. "Can my fish go too?"

"Don't be stupid," he said.

I flinched.

"Mommy will take care of it, okay?" Dad was talking real fast. That's how I knew he was lying.

"Mommy's not going with us?"

Dad got up and walked over to my closet. He grabbed my jacket, the one with the furry hood. It wasn't even cold outside.

"Put this on." He shoved it at me.

"Why can't Mommy go too?"

He plopped the heavy jacket on my shoulders. "We're playing a game," he said, guiding my arm through the sleeve. "It's like hide and seek. But you have to be quiet, okay? Don't make any noise. Not one word."

"But why?" I asked.

"Because I said so." He grabbed my backpack and stuffed my pillow inside it, punching it down with his fist.

I followed him through the hallway into the living room. The house looked like somebody turned it upside-down and shook it. Beer bottles tipped on the floor. A chair knocked over, as if it fell and gave up. Broken glass sprayed across the carpet. Mom was slumped on the couch, her legs twisted at a weird angle. When I moved toward her, Dad pulled me away.

"She's sleeping," he told me.

I looked back at Mom. Her long dark hair spread out across

the floor like the Virgin Mary's halo on the candles under the sink.

Dad scooped his car keys off the table. "Grab your shoes." He motioned for me to hurry.

I dug through the pile of sneakers in the hallway.

"Not your flip-flops."

"But I don't want my sneakers."

"Now." Dad yanked the laces so tight, my foot throbbed.

As we moved through the kitchen, he grabbed a knife off the counter. A big one.

"What's that for?" I asked.

"Don't worry about it," he said, unlocking the front door. "No more questions. We've got to hurry, okay?" He grabbed my hand and tugged me onto the porch.

As we stepped outside, a light clicked on.

"Shit," he muttered.

The light above the porch keeps away the bad guys. That's what Dad told me. But it was just a stupid lamp. How could it keep us safe?

I stumbled across the grass. When we reached the truck, Dad yanked open the passenger door and tossed my backpack on the seat.

"Get in," he said.

A flashlight cut across the lawn—Mr. Mendoza, walking his bony old mutt, Rico, in the middle of the night.

"Everything okay?" he called out.

I shook my head.

Dad pushed me inside the truck, then he ran to the driver's side and got behind the wheel. The engine roared to life. He didn't even turn on the headlights. We lurched forward, bumping across the front yard. The light above the porch faded away. I tipped my face against the window and thought about my guppies, their mouths at the surface of the tank, gasping for breath.

4

On Monday, I'm on the PE field picking up garbage. This is my third lunch detention so far this semester. Three strikes you're out. My crime? Missing half of first period French. When your primary mode of transportation is a city bus, you're going to be late.

Why should I bother going to class? Par-lay voo fran-say. All that shit we're forced to memorize like robots. I mean, what's the freaking point? Let's be real. I'm not flying to Paris unless I win big at scratch-off. It's a waste of time just dreaming about it.

Do I dream about it?

Oui.

It's not my fault I'm late all the time. I used to have a really sweet mountain bike, but Dad sold it on eBay for a hundred bucks. Who am I kidding? I've never been to the mountains. The only hill I've ever seen is Mount Trashmore, a landfill off the Florida turnpike.

The PE field is loaded with dead trees. Their roots bend toward the sky as if they're growing in reverse. A goal post toppled over during a hurricane last summer, but the bleachers are still there. That's the way storms work. They take what they want and leave the rest behind.

When detention's finally over, I swing by the vending machines. All your basic food groups arranged by color. Purple soda. Yellow popcorn. Stale crackers and orange sludge, the kind that comes with a tiny plastic shovel.

I slide my thumb inside the coin slot and flick out a couple of quarters. Sweet. You never know when you're going to get lucky. Cash shows up in the weirdest places. One time, I found twenty bucks taped inside a sneaker at Goodwill. Me and Dad spent it all on Grand Slams at Denny's because sometimes the best thing for dinner is breakfast. Man, that was an awesome day.

If we're really desperate for cash, we go out and hunt for cans behind the school. It's kind of embarrassing, so I always wear my stanky black hoodie and pray nobody recognizes me. We stuff our Hefty bags until they're ready to burst and dump them at the recycling center. You'd be surprised how much it adds up. One time, we got thirty bucks for two bags. No joke.

I used to tie the Coke tabs to my shoelaces and jingle-stomp to class. I thought about making a prom dress out of those metal tabs. That would be so amazing. Then Chad Skinner started calling them "slut badges" and I never wore them again.

My stomach clenches. I'm so used to feeling hungry all the time, I can almost tune it out. It's like background noise. In middle school, Dad used to drop me off early so I could get the free breakfast. Usually, it was a hard-boiled egg, a muffin, and chocolate milk. I like soft-boiled, but hard's better than nothing.

The bell rings and a tide of bodies surges against me. Everybody's in a big rush to go to class and sit at a desk for the next forty-five minutes. I take my time, sliding quarters into the vending machine. Sugar first. Then quadratic equations.

I cram a handful of M&Ms in my mouth and chew real slow. Last night, I didn't eat dinner. Dad was so freaked out. I still can't believe he hit me. That's never happened before. Not even when I was a kid. I think he liked me better when I was little. When I couldn't fight back.

If he doesn't find a job soon, the fun's just beginning. Dad's good at finding crap jobs. He's not so good at sticking to them, and besides, they never pay enough. It doesn't matter how hard he works. When you're making eight bucks an hour, it won't go far.

I slept on the bathroom floor. In the morning, Dad was gone. What's going to happen when I get back to the motel? Maybe he'll freak out again. Or maybe he'll act like everything's cool. Dad's acting skills are on point. He should win an Oscar or something.

For once, I don't want school to end. I lean against the vending machine and stare at the fire alarm bolted to the stairs.

PUSH

THEN PULL

It's probably been there a million years. Did anybody ever try to pull it? The school's got cameras everywhere. Real high-tech stuff. I swear, those cameras must be invisible because I've never seen any.

A bunch of freshmen girls make a last-minute run for the bathroom, laughing as if they've got a VIP party in there. Right now I could care less. I'm sick of following everybody else's rules. I reach up and grab the fire alarm's T-shaped handle. Push, then pull.

Lights stutter around the hallway as the alarm drills my skull. I'm just standing there like an idiot. It would look weird if I started running, so I plop down on a bench and watch the classroom doors swing open, one by one.

Mr. Fordham pokes his head out of the band room. I'm surprised he can hear anything after the alarm finally shuts up. He's probably a hundred years old. Maybe he's got special hearing like a dog that can sense noises beyond human range. For example, my heart slamming against my ribs.

"Leave your instruments on your chairs," he yells.

I hate the way he says *instruments*. It sounds nasty. Maybe he thinks we're on lockdown, a kid trying to shoot up the school or whatever. I can't even explain why I pulled that alarm. I just needed to be in control of something, if only for a limited time.

"Get in line, people. Move. What if this was a real fire?" Mr. Fordham claps his hands.

Okay, I'm moving.

As I push through the hallway, I notice this extra-tall boy sort of bopping along with the crowd. Shawn. He's wearing that stupid Lifeguard T-shirt again. Today it's under a floppy cargo jacket with lots of pockets. I bet he actually carries stuff in it. Swiss army knives. Maybe a hand grenade. I shove my way past the flute girls and rush up to him. When I tap his arm, he turns around.

"What if this was a real fire?" he says.

"If this was a real fire, we'd be dead."

Shawn tugs up his hood like a ninja on a secret mission. "That's a comforting thought."

"The entire school's made of concrete. I guess some of us could survive."

"You're forgetting one minor detail."

"What's that?" I ask.

"I'd be here to rescue you," he says, grinning.

Right. This skinny kid with a retainer is going to rescue me.

"I can rescue myself."

"Balls to the wall. That's more your style."

"Is that supposed to be a compliment?"

"I don't give out compliments very often. Not the sincere kind anyway. So who pulled the alarm?"

I look away. "Maybe it went off by itself."

"Yeah," he says. "It does that sometimes."

"It does?"

"I bet the school's going to dust it for fingerprints."

"You mean call the cops?"

He nods. "It's a federal offense."

"It is?" Now I'm starting to get scared.

"Yep. Class one misdemeanor."

"But I'm only sixteen."

Shit.

Did I just say that out loud?

He smirks. "No worries, Miss Balls-To-The-Wall. Unless you've already spent time behind bars, your fingerprints don't exist."

I really hope that's true.

When we reach the front entrance, Shawn holds the door open for me. Okay, that was sort of sweet. I can't remember the last time anyone did that. Everybody's standing on a trampled patch of grass near the chain-link fence—a safe distance from the non-existent fire. I dig inside my pocket and give him what's left of the M&Ms.

"I saved you the green ones."

"Awesome," he says, tilting the bag into his mouth. "I always eat two at the same time so they won't be lonely."

"That's very considerate of you."

"Yeah, I know. Can I shoot you a question?"

"Shoot away."

"So that motel. Is that, like, your permanent home?"

I flinch. "Did somebody tell you that?"

"I sort of figured it out when I saw your dad."

Now what am I supposed to do? I could make up a lie, but it's too late for that. I stare at the red plastic cups jammed into the fence. From here, it spells DARE. Up close, it just looks like garbage.

"Yeah, that's where I live." No use lying about it. God, I've never told anyone before. Why am I telling Shawn? I mean, why do I think I can trust him? And I want to trust him. Trust somebody.

Dad's going to kill me.

"Hey, I was just curious. I'm not judging you, I swear," says Shawn. "At least you get free soap, right?"

"We don't get free anything."

"Not even those little plastic shampoo bottles?"

I don't wash my hair with shampoo. Dad says it's a waste of money. We use plain old soap for everything—the cheapest we can find at the Dollar Store.

"Please don't go spreading this around," I tell Shawn.

"No worries. Your secret's safe with me."

For a moment, we don't say anything.

"You've been there a while?" he asks.

Last summer, I was living in a van. How embarrassing is this?

"We sort of moved around a lot."

"Ah, I get it," he says. "You were on the run."

I reach inside my Hail Kale bag for my menthols. They taste

like pine needles dipped in bleach, but I don't care. Smoking gives me a reason to keep quiet. And right now, I'm talking too much.

"You forgot this." He reaches into his jacket and takes out a lighter. My lighter, actually.

"Thanks." I shove it in my bag. For some reason, I don't feel like smoking anymore.

The bell clangs. Time to crawl back to our zoo cages. Mr. Fordham stomps toward us, waving his arms like he's chopping wood.

"Get in line, people," he yells, but everybody's moving in clumps of twos and threes.

Shawn's walking so close, I can smell the soap on his skin, something clean and sweet. Cut grass. Or the baseball field after it rains. He brushes up against my arm, startling me.

"Did it hurt?" he asks.

For a second, I think he's making fun of my Stain. Why not? Everybody else does. Then he taps his lower lip.

"Oh," I say, a little embarrassed. "You mean my piercings?"

Here's how it went down.

Me and Dad got wasted last summer. We knocked back a couple of Bud Lights. I marked the spot on my lower lip with a ballpoint pen. Held my breath. Pinched the skin so tight, I almost passed out.

"Yeah," I tell Shawn. "It hurt like hell."

I push my way toward the school's front entrance. Shawn's already headed inside. He slings his backpack over his shoulder.

"Catch you later, snake bite," he says, giving me a salute like we're marching into battle.

I watch him disappear. Now he knows my secret. It didn't seem like a big deal to him. Maybe he was just trying to be nice. I don't know. It's kind of rare that anybody's nice to me.

Before I head inside the building, I glance over my shoulder. Call it instinct or whatever. There's a man leaning against the chain-link fence. He's just standing there, arms folded over his chest. Definitely not a teacher.

He's a cop.

Not the rent-a-cop the school hired to sleep in the parking lot. No badge, no uniform. Still, I have no doubt this guy's a cop. How do I know? Because I've been hiding from cops all my life.

I study the thick, beaded chain around the guy's neck. He's probably got his badge hidden under his shirt. That's another thing. The "look" they're going for. Usually, a jeans-and-tee combo. No labels. Clean sneakers. Too clean, in fact.

Did he show up here because of the fire alarm? No, there wasn't enough time. He must've been on campus already. Doing what? I have no clue. He must be looking for something. Or someone.

Is he looking for me?

As much as I want to run, I take it nice and slow. When I glance back, the campus is empty. One minute the cop's there. Then he's gone. How could someone just drop off the face of the earth as if they never existed?

I wouldn't know.

5

Class has finally ended. By the time I reach the bus stop, I'm out of breath. I keep glancing over my shoulder, looking for that cop, but there's no sign of him.

A woman eases onto the bench. She's got freckles smeared all over her arms and a tattoo of a rosary scraped into her ankle. Without thinking, I scoot over. Don't want to get too close, in case she tries to steal something off me.

"It's late." She squints at the bus sign.

I shrug like I've gone deaf and watch a plastic bag tumble and flatten against a tree. I swear, it feels like the trees are fighting a war with all things plastic. And the plastic is winning.

Hurry up, bus.

Finally, it wheezes up to the curb. God, that took forever. The door flaps open and a bunch of old people stumble out. I push my way inside and tap my EASY card against the box.

"No good," the driver says.

My card's out of money. Now what am I supposed to do? I reach in my Hail Kale bag and dig around for change. I've got a couple of nickels. A penny so old, it turned green. That's it.

A hand stretches out and plunks a quarter into the slot.

My new friend, the tattoo lady.

"Thanks," I mumble.

❧

The Surfside is quiet after I get home from school. Home. What a joke. I'm supposed to be thankful we're in a real place now. If I had the keys, I'd be camping in the van tonight. At least I'd have a little space to myself.

I head upstairs, keeping an eye out for tweakers. It's scary as hell walking around the motel by myself. You never know what's going to pop up. Or who. I march past the rows of numbered rooms, keeping my head down low.

The door next to our room is propped open. That's weird. I peek inside and some random dude blinks back at me. He's got a Band-Aid stuck to his chin and he's shirtless above his jeans.

"Hi there, blondie," he says, grinning. "How much?"

I walk a little faster.

Somebody left a half-empty beer bottle on the ledge outside our room. Nice. I'm already bracing myself for a rage-fest. This is going to suck on multiple levels. It doesn't even smell like Dad's frying up dinner.

I shove the key in the lock. The door swings open so fast, it bangs against the wall. The room's pitch black, which really freaks me out. Never walk into a dark room. That's one of Dad's major rules.

Okay. Here goes. I smack the light switch and peek inside. Everything looks the same. In other words, just as crappy as it did yesterday. My socks and undies dripping over the shower rod. The "tropical" bedspread crumpled in a heap. Palm trees and coconuts. I haven't seen one damn coconut since we got here.

I dump my Hail Kale bag on the floor and click on the TV. Guess it's cuisine à la microwave tonight. It takes exactly five minutes to nuke one of Dad's Salisbury steak dinners. The mashed potatoes always get stuck in my throat like Elmer's glue. I swallow that part first and save the gritty meat for last. It's like chewing a hamburger, minus the bun.

This place is way too quiet.

Where the hell is Dad? I need to tell him about Mr. Plain White Tee. There must be a reason that cop showed up at school. If he's looking for me, why now? He must've had a clue, but it's been years since I disappeared. I was just a little kid. Did something happen? That's what I'm going to find out.

I sit on my mattress next to the bed, chewing Salisbury steak and scratching the bug bites on my ankle. Today I woke up with more welts. Three in a row. Breakfast, lunch, and dinner. They never go after Dad. Maybe his blood's too sour.

He should be here by now.

The guy next door is yelling at his girlfriend. So much for quiet. I can hear every four-letter word through the cheap dry-wall. In a couple hours, they'll forget whatever bullshit they were screaming about and start having sex. Loudly. I don't know which noise is worse.

I crank up the TV and watch this brain-dead show about vacation homes. Seriously. That's all it is. Rich people hunting for wood-burning ovens in big-ass mansions where they never cook. I kind of wish they'd burst into flames. Now that would be something worth watching.

I'm halfway to dreamland when the door bangs open and Dad stumbles into the room. I can already tell he's wasted. No big surprise. I'm used to him knocking back a few Bud Lights after sundown. Yeah, that's what I expected.

Here's what I didn't expect.

It takes me a second to recognize his hiccupy laugh. The frayed leather jacket. The smile that doesn't quite reach both sides of his face. He's worse than a sky rat. Actually, he's just a regular rat.

Booth.

What's he doing here? No doubt, he wants something. He's probably breathing down Dad's neck about the rent. We've been living in this dump since last summer. You'd think he'd give us a break, right? Fat chance.

Booth eases onto the mattress next to me. I'm so grossed out, I can't even breathe. "Hello, young lady," he says, wiggling his fingers. "Remember me?"

What does he expect me to say? I remember you promised to kick us out the next time you caught us "stealing" from the dumpster.

Yeah, I remember you.

I stare at the patches on his stupid jacket. "Why are you here?"

"Reece." Dad narrows his eyes at me.

Booth must be high or something because he smiles and pats my shoulder. He's one of those touchy-feely types. No concept of personal space. "So how do you like it here? Been spending a lot of time at the beach?"

Right. I go to the beach every day. Get my tan on. Party with Drake on his yacht. That kind of thing. I need to tell Dad about the cop I saw at school, but I can't say anything if Booth's hanging around.

I grab my Hail Kale bag and head for the door. "Peace out."

Dad's up in my face, breathing King of Beer fumes all over me. "Hold on. You're not going anywhere."

"But I need to finish my paper. It's due tomorrow."

"You've had plenty of time to work on that. Why did you wait this long?"

"I didn't know we were having guests," I say, glaring at Booth.

"Watch your attitude." Dad's getting fired up, blasting straight into the Rage Zone.

Booth shoves his gut between us. "It's all right, Jay," he says, pushing him. Jay my ass. I don't even know Dad's real name. He changes it every time we move. "If she wants to go, let her go."

This guy's been here five minutes and he's already trying to act like my dad. I've had enough of that crap, thank you. He just wants me out of this room so I don't block his game. I get the feeling he's up to something.

Dad lets go. I squeeze past him before he changes his mind and the door slams shut behind me. If he's taking sides with Booth, I'm in trouble. It's supposed to be me and Dad against the world. That's the way it's always been.

He's never taken somebody else's side before.

I sit on the concrete ledge outside the motel room. The fluorescent lights buzz and flicker, throwing out a sickly green light. I can barely read my crumpled paper. "In Greek mythology, it really sucks if you're a girl. You might have to turn into a tree or something to avoid getting jumped..."

I can't work on this stupid essay now. What the hell was I thinking? It's due tomorrow and I've barely even started. I scrunch up the paper. God, this is so stupid. I should have a real desk. And a bed. Normal things for a normal life.

Screw this.

I get up and press my ear against the door. Yeah, I'm acting like a freak, but right now I'm sort of desperate.

"Your rent's way past due," Booth is saying.

"Please," Dad says. "Can't we work something out? I just need a little more time."

I hate the way he's begging. It really makes me sick.

"You've had enough time."

"Just give me a few more days."

Booth doesn't say anything for a moment. "Okay," he says, like he's Mr. Nice Guy. "You've got until the end of the week. I know it must be tough. I'm a father too. But your little girl's not so little anymore."

"Yeah," Dad agrees. "That's the problem."

"What about her mother?"

"She's out of the picture," Dad says.

I rub my eyes, but the sting won't go away.

When we moved down to Miami, I really hoped things would be different this time. Dad would score a decent job. We'd finally save up enough for a real place. I'd stay in high school long enough to graduate. Then what? Go to college and study dinosaurs? I can't even think about the future. It's like wishing on birthday candles, the kind that fizzle and spark no matter how many times you blow them out.

A door swings open at the end of the breezeway. Room 22. Out pops Mouse, dragging her Barbie by the hair.

I quickly wipe my face and put on a fake smile. "Hey, what's up?"

Mouse is definitely on a mission. She's got one of those plastic bubble wands and she's blowing on it so hard, it doesn't stand a chance.

"Here," I say, crouching beside her on the steps. "You're going to pop a lung. Let me show you how."

She gives it another shot. When a chain of bubbles shoots out of that wand, Mouse is so thrilled, she starts jumping up and down. God, I can't remember ever feeling that excited about some damn soap.

The lady with the plastic curlers is watching like always. She pokes her frizzy head out of the room, as if she's scared of the dark, but there are worse things than darkness in this motel.

"Come here," she yells.

Mouse darts back inside the motel room.

Bam!

They're gone.

All of a sudden, it hits me. That little girl isn't her kid. Why didn't I see it before? That crazy lady's a lot older than Dad. Her mouth is creased with lines, as if she's spent her whole life frowning. She's always got her feet crammed into high heels, though I never see her go anywhere. Her chunky earrings remind me of Fruit Loops, one green, one blue.

It's bad enough living in a motel when you're a grown-ass adult. I can't imagine how it feels for Mouse. Then again, maybe she's got it better than me. At least she doesn't know what she's missing.

I lean against the concrete wall. My head throbs. This day has been one massive suck. Dad begging for more time and kissing Booth's ass. The cop showing up at school. And now Shawn knows my secret. He probably thinks it's weird that I'm living in a motel. I bet he won't talk to me again. Even Fruit Loop won't talk to me. Why is she so scared?

She thinks I'm a sky rat.

That's why.

The motel room's door flings open and Booth stumbles out. He almost trips over me on his way toward the stairs.

"Have fun," he says, winking at me.

Loser.

I go back inside the room. Dad's passed out on the bed, snoring like a brontosaurus. The TV's blasting an old black-and-white movie. Lots of gunfire and people falling on the ground. Not a speck of blood. That's the thing about old movies. They leave the hard stuff out.

I step over the beer cans scattered on the floor. Nice job, Dad. I squeeze his shoulder, trying to get him to wake up.

"Dad," I shout at him.

He opens his eyes. "You're back."

Yeah, that's kind of obvious.

"Are we getting kicked out?" I ask him.

"Not yet," he says, clicking off the TV. "Got us a little more time."

"What did you do?"

I'm almost afraid to ask.

"Just gave him a little down payment. That's all."

"What's that supposed to mean?"

He doesn't answer.

I should tell him about the cop. Instead, I stretch out on my mattress on the floor and throw the blanket over my head. If Dad's going to keep secrets from me…well, I can do the same. Besides. I'm probably getting worked up about nothing.

At least, that's what I hope.

6

We ditched the truck and headed into the woods. Why did we have to get out and walk? And why wasn't Mommy here too? The trees swayed against the moonless sky, their branches scraping the dark.

"Just a little further," Dad told me.

I didn't recognize the shape of the pines. I'd never been so far away. Never seen my dad so angry. Sure, he and Mom got into a lot of fights. Sometimes he took off for a couple days, but he always came home.

Dad shrugged off his backpack. He reached inside and took out the kitchen knife. The blade glinted in the moonlight.

"Stay still," he said.

I squeezed my eyes shut.

He grabbed my braid and pulled. My chin tilted up, as if I was counting stars. The blade swooped against my neck so close, I thought he'd cut me. Still, I didn't scream. I knew better.

My braid dropped into the weeds. I reached up and touched bare skin. He didn't ask. He just did it anyway. I wanted to grow it long. Even longer than the Little Mermaid's hair.

"Why did you cut it off?" I screamed.

Dad scooped up the braid and crammed it in his pocket. "Listen," he said. "You have to be brave, okay? The bad guys are looking for us."

"What bad guys?" I was choking back sobs.

"It's like hide-and-seek," he told me.

That's a game for babies.

He tucked a strand of hair behind my ear. "Can you be brave?"

I shook my head.

He waved at the trees, as if the bad guys were up there, hiding in the branches. In my mind, they were shadows with glowing red eyes. "If they find us, they'll take you away. Then you'll never see me again."

I shivered.

Dad crouched next to me. "Be brave, needle legs." He kissed my cheek. "From now on, you're going to be a boy."

A boy?

"I know this is scary," he told me. "Just think of it like a game. You're good at pretending. That's why Miss Garcia put you in that play at school."

In the Christmas pageant, I was a lamb. Me and all the other girls. We glued cotton balls to brown paper grocery bags. I knelt at the edge of stage, watching Andrew Bilski punch holes in his sneaker with a paper clip.

"Why do I have to be a boy?"

"It's safer that way. Your hair will grow back," he said, stroking my neck. "Then you can be a girl again."

It didn't make any sense. What's so safe about being a boy?

My backpack swayed against my shoulders. I wanted to take it off. Throw it in the bushes. Let it rot with the squirrel bones I found there. When we reached a stream, Dad took my braid out of his pocket. He untied the rubber band and tossed it away. My hair floated on the surface of the water, drifting in circles like my fish. Then it was gone and so was my name.

That night we slept in the tent. We crunched through apples and granola bars, but my stomach wouldn't stop burning. The pines tipped above us, their branches creaking secret music.

"When are we going home?" I asked.

Dad glared. "Remember what I told you?"

I remembered.

The bad guys are looking for us.

He told me that the raccoon crumpled on the road was sleeping. If I swallowed a piece of gum, it would stay tangled inside me forever. The stain above my eye is where the angels kissed me before I was born.

"Nobody's going to hurt you," he said, squeezing my hand under the blanket. "Not if we're together."

"What if the bad guys find me?"

"You know what to do."

T-Rex.

We'd gone over it a million times. If I was in trouble, that's what I was supposed to say. The magic code word.

T-Rex. T-Rex. T-Rex.

I whispered it over and over until it made no sense. Then Dad got up and unzipped the tent and I started to panic.

"Where are you going?" I whispered.

He twisted around. "Gotta drain the tank. Be right back," he said, all jumpy. "Want to play a game with me?"

I nodded.

"Can you count to a hundred?"

A hundred is a lot of zeroes.

I counted inside my head. One Mississippi. Two Mississippi. Now I was really scared. We had to stick together. Isn't that what Dad said? I had to go too, but I didn't want to pee in the dark. Not if the bad guys were out there looking for me.

After a long time, Dad finally came back to the tent. He was sweating and his jeans were soaking wet, as if he'd gone for a swim. He looked worried. I'd never seen my dad that nervous before.

I threw my arms around him. "Did you find the bad guys?"

"Not yet, needle legs," he said, holding me tight.

I listened to the night noises swirling above the tent. Crickets scraping their wings. The stream where my hair floated away. The trees listening to me. All of a sudden, there was something I needed to ask.

"Is Mommy a bad guy too?"

For a moment, he was quiet.

"Your mother's dead." His voice cracked into a sob.

That's how I knew he was telling the truth.

7

I lift my head off the desk. Mrs. Colby's erasing the board, her arm swishing back and forth. The room's empty, as if the school's been wiped out by a killer comet. No survivors. Did I fall asleep in class?

Of course, I did.

If I don't jet out of here, I'm going to miss my bus. This is beyond embarrassing. I grab my Hail Kale bag and march to the front of the room. We're supposed to leave our research papers on her desk. Mine's only a page, so I shove it at the bottom of the pile and hope she doesn't notice.

"Reece?" Mrs. Colby holds up my crumpled paper. "Is this your essay?"

I glance around the classroom. A plastic skeleton in a dusty robe is slumped against the cabinets. It has something to do with the special people in the Spirit Club and their Homecoming float. It seems like throwing parties is all they do.

"Yeah, it's mine."

"I'm sorry," she says, flipping the page over, as if there's more written on the back. Unfortunately, there isn't. "I can't accept handwritten work."

How am I supposed to type that stupid paper? Teachers always say, "If you don't have a computer at home, go to the library." Yeah, right. Are you going to pay for my bus ticket or drive me there?

"Sorry it's kind of a mess. I didn't have time to finish last night."

Mrs. Colby frowns. "Then maybe you should've started working on it earlier."

Wow. I never thought of that.

"Can we chat for a second?" she asks, sinking into her chair. She actually sounds worried. Mrs. Colby's okay, as far as teachers go, except her name reminds me of cheese and she's got this weird obsession with basset hounds. Her coffee mug is decorated with dogs in goofy-looking hats. They all have the same idiotic expression, as if they're thrilled to be wearing bonnets.

I glance at the clock above her desk. I'm late. The bus probably left without me. "I really have to go."

"Just a minute," she says.

I take a seat.

In language arts, we've been reading about Greek mythology. This class is kind of boring, but, like I said, I'll read anything. Mrs. Colby blabs on about symbolism and metaphors and I skip ahead to the good parts. My favorite goddess is Medusa. When I saw her picture (not her real picture, duh. A sculpture in a museum or something), I thought her snaky hair looked pretty badass.

If only I could turn myself into stone.

"It's a shame." Mrs. Colby smoothes the creases in my paper. "Your in-class essays are strong, but you're falling behind on homework."

I could tell the truth. I didn't finish that stupid paper because I was too busy trying to sleep while the guy next door screamed his head off.

"I'm just going through some stuff."

The magic word.

Stuff could mean anything. It stops teachers from asking too many questions. Works every time.

At least, until now.

"Something you want to talk about?" she asks hopefully.

No, I don't want to talk about it.

I stare at the smiling hounds on her coffee mug. "I'll do better next time."

"Really?" she says. "To be honest, I'm a little concerned. You fell asleep at your desk today."

Well, it's a lot more comfortable than the floor.

"It won't happen again. I swear."

Mrs. Colby sighs. "Reece, you haven't been yourself lately."

I choke back a laugh.

Mrs. Colby thinks I haven't been myself?

She's right.

"I'm just tired." I shift my feet. The crusty layer of glue inside my boot digs against my bug-bitten ankle. I must be losing my mind because for a nano-second, I feel like telling Mrs. Colby everything.

In second grade, I told my teacher, Mr. Branson, that I fell off my bike and my skull had been throbbing for days (true). Dad wouldn't take me to a doctor (also true) unless it was a real emergency. Then we'd have to wait in the emergency room because we had no insurance. Mr. Branson freaked out and called my dad.

"Can't leave my shift at the restaurant," Dad mumbled on the phone. "Just pop an aspirin or something."

Mr. Branson walked me to the nurse's office. We played Go Fish until Dad showed up hours later.

I used to pretend Mr. Branson was my real dad.

When I fell off the monkey bars and skinned my knee, Dad patched it up with Super Glue. When he slammed his finger in the door, he wrapped it in a popsicle stick and duct tape. If my tooth hurts, I pray it goes away. Fast. Dad's already lost a molar. I yanked it out with a pair of pliers. He was spitting blood for days.

"Nobody's going to look back there anyway," he said, laughing.

Who cares if nobody sees?

I know his mouth is full of holes.

"This is starting to become a habit." Mrs. Colby scrunches her eyebrows. "Is something going on at home?"

Every time I switch schools, it's the same thing. Teachers always want to know what's going on at home.

"Nothing. I'm fine."

Mrs. Colby doesn't look convinced. "I can offer a one-day extension on the research paper. How does that sound?"

"Sounds good." I start fast-walking toward the door. Hard

to believe she's giving me a choice. I wasn't even allowed to pick my own topic. This is a big waste of my time. I need to catch the bus before it takes off.

"If you don't finish your paper by tomorrow, I'll have to give you a zero," she calls out. "That's a big chunk of your grade."

What does she expect me to do? Bow down at her desk? There's no such thing as zero. It's not even a number. Just empty space. Mrs. Colby has no clue. I've got bigger problems than Odysseus.

I push through the hallway and slam my weight against the double doors, then I'm outside, breathing the non-air-conditioned air. The seniors are already drifting across the field. Why do they always get out first? I guess it's easy when you never go to class.

Sure enough, the bus is long gone. I sink down on the bench and drop my head between my knees. I don't want to walk to the motel like a crazy hitchhiker in my busted-ass boots. There's no place I really want to go.

I just don't want to be.

If atoms are mostly empty space, I can't think of anything emptier than my subatomic particles.

I glance across the PE field, searching for that cop. I scan the empty bleachers. No sign of Mr. Plain White Tee. The parking lot's a wasteland. Just when I start to breathe easy, I spot him leaning against the chain-link fence.

"Hey, snake bite."

I turn around. There's Shawn, marching across the grass. He's still wearing that stupid jacket, the one with all the pockets. I bet he's got a car. Or a ride home. Unfortunately, these are things I don't have.

The cop is watching us now. There's nothing I can do. If I go back inside the school, I'm trapped. It's better to stay out in the open. I take a deep breath and start walking over to Shawn.

"Are you shouting at me?"

"Not shouting," he says. "Just talking loud."

"That's what I thought."

He laughs. It's really sweet, the way he laughs so easily. Most guys try to act cool all the time. "How's it going?" he asks.

"My bus took off."

Stupid, stupid, stupid.

"You mean, like just now?"

"I guess so." It's not like I was recording it with a hidden camera.

"That sucks. So what are you going to do?"

"Walk home, I guess."

Home.

Shawn knows I live in a crappy motel. It didn't seem like a big deal to him. Still, I'm embarrassed. I glance back at the chain-link fence. The cop's still there, keeping an eye on us.

"You need a ride?" Shawn asks.

"Sure," I say, a little too quickly. "If you've got transportation."

"I left my DeLorean in storage. My sister's Honda will have to do. Is that okay?"

Wait. Shawn has a sister?

"Yeah, it's okay," I tell him. "In fact, it's more than okay."

"Wow. That's even better than regular okay. That's like super unleaded okay."

We walk through the maze of parked cars. I try to think of something funny to make him laugh again, but my brain isn't working right now.

Before I can say anything, a hand drops between us. I look up and there's a girl attached to the hand.

"Thanks for making me wait," she tells Shawn. "I've been sweating out here forever."

"That's scientifically impossible," he says, shaking his head. "You were probably waiting ten, maybe fifteen minutes."

"And that's why you're walking home." She tilts her gaze in my direction. "Who are you?"

"I'm Reece." It slips out so easily, you'd think I was born with this name.

"Well, hello, Reece," she says, sliding a gold bracelet up and down her arm. "Are you hanging out with my little brother by choice? Or bad luck?"

"Be nice, Emily. The bus left without her," he says.

"That definitely counts as bad luck." Emily stares at me so intensely, I want to dig through the concrete and bury myself in the parking lot. Her cheekbones are tanned like Shawn's, but her eyes are so pale it's startling.

Shawn grabs the keys out of her hand. "My turn."

"Don't even try that," she says.

He's already marching to the car. When he said, "Honda," I thought he meant something small. Not this beast. "Let me drive the Tank," he says, sliding behind the wheel. "Remember what Mom said? I need practice."

"You're right about the practice part." She gets in the backseat and crosses her blue-jeaned legs like a queen in a chariot.

Guess I'm riding shotgun.

As I open the passenger door, I look back at the chain-link fence. The cop isn't there anymore. At first, I think he's gone. Then I see him on the baseball field, watching us from the bleachers. How did he get there so fast? It's like he's got super-powers or something. I fight the urge to glance back again. I can't let Mr. Plain White Tee know that I'm watching him too.

The Tank's got that ultra-clean, never-been-used smell. I bet the seats are real leather. God, I've never been in a car this nice before. The dashboard lights up like a spaceship. I didn't even know cars had computer screens. What are you supposed to do with it? Post a selfie?

"Don't crash, okay?" Emily tells her brother.

He's already gunning it out of the parking lot. "I make no promises."

As we pull away from school, I watch the grey slab of a building fade into the distance. I can't remember the last time I rode in a car with somebody else. Right now, it doesn't even matter where I'm going.

I'm free.

8

Every time I moved someplace new, I didn't really see anything. I saw dirty motel rooms that faced the highway. Empty lots snarled with barbed wire. Fire escapes where strings of laundry flapped like flags in the breeze.

To be honest, I didn't see much.

I'm seeing it now.

Shawn's driving around, giving me a little tour. The water's right next to us—a burst of light and color flashing between the tall buildings. I didn't know it was so close. I probably could've walked there from the motel. When I stare at the waves sparkling in the sunlight, I can't help wondering what else I've missed.

"Is that the ocean?" I ask.

"Not exactly," he says. "I mean, it's not the white sand and palm trees kind of beach you see on TV. The bay's fun for kayaking, though. Especially when you're cruising through the mangrove tunnels."

"Mangroves?"

"See those big trees?" he says, pointing out the window. "Their roots grow above the water like stilts. You know what's really cool? Mangrove seeds float all over the world. Those trees could've swam here all the way from India."

"That's so amazing. I thought trees were stuck in the ground. I didn't know they traveled like that."

He laughs. "Traveling trees. That's what I'm going to name my band."

"You're in a band?"

"Not yet. But give me time."

We're both laughing again. This is officially the best drive ever. I'm having so much fun cruising around with Shawn and his uber-cool sister, I almost forgot that I'm supposed to be back at the motel. Then my phone buzzes and I'm not laughing anymore.

Shawn nudges me. "Hey, your phone's blowing up."

I really don't want to talk to Dad right now. It's way too embarrassing. If I don't pick up, he'll just keep calling over and over like a psycho. I reach into my Hail Kale bag and dig out my phone.

Emily peers over my seat. "Whoa. Your phone's so old school."

Please God. Just kill me now. Where's a killer comet when you need one? I mash the phone against my ear. Dad's blabbing at warp speed, going off about his favorite subject, the rules.

"Where are you?" He's in full-on rage mode. "Why aren't you at the motel? You know the rules."

I want to tell him about the cop, but I can't right now. Not in front of Shawn. I take a deep breath. "The bus took off without me."

"What do you mean, 'took off'?"

"It was at school. Now it's gone."

"I got that part. Are you on the next bus?"

I'm seriously thinking about lying to Dad. I don't even feel guilty about it. Well, maybe a teensy bit guilty. What if he shows up at the bus stop and I'm not there? I've never broken the rules like this before.

"Yeah, I'm on my way."

"You better be," he snaps. "When you get back, we're going to have a little talk. Maybe I need to refresh your memory about the rules."

I'm sick of Dad's rules.

It's time I made my own.

Let him worry about me for a change. I wipe my sweaty palms on my jeans and hope Shawn doesn't notice. He's looking at the road, but he must sense it.

"Let me guess," he says. "Your dad's freaking out."

I turn off the phone and shove it in my bag. "I should wear a GPS tracker or something."

"My dad's crazy like that too."

"Yeah?" I try to smile.

Crazy isn't the word for my dad. Why can't I have a little space to myself? Just once in my life, I want to be normal like everybody else. I never had the chance. Dad made sure of that. Still, I can't help feeling like I've let him down. I lean against the window, as if I'm going to be sick.

Shawn taps my arm. "You want to hang at my place for a while? Just until things cool off?"

Things are never going to "cool off." Not as long as I'm stuck in Dad's twisted version of reality. God, I'm in so much trouble right now. I've never gone to a boy's house before. Dad's going to kill me. I'm breaking the rules on multiple levels. No joke. I can't remember the last time I went anywhere by myself.

Shawn's looking at me, waiting for my answer.

"Okay," I tell him.

Let's go.

ॐ

As we speed over the causeway to Key Biscayne, I hold my breath. I don't want Shawn to know that water isn't my thing. The bay churns below us, the waves dented with foam.

"What are those tall buildings?" I ask.

"That's downtown. You've never been there before?"

"No," I say, a little embarrassed. As the bridge slopes down, I glance at the trees beside the road and spot a peacock dragging its tail.

Most people don't realize that birds are just dinosaurs with feathers. Somehow they survived the killer comet. Their birdy-genes mutated so they could sing. The same genes that gave humans vocal cords. We have that much in common.

Shawn squeezes my knee. "You're spacing out again."

"Sorry," I tell him. "I didn't eat anything today."

"You should probably fix that."

"If only it were that easy."

Emily laughs. "So where are you from, Reece?"

In my mind, I flash on all the places I've lived. The tent in the pines where the trees listened to me. Motel rooms in nameless cities. The backseat of the van. And now Miami, where I've never seen the ocean.

"I moved around a lot."

That's what Dad taught me to say. Not exactly a lie, but not the whole truth. The less I explain, the better.

"You're, like, interrogating her," says Shawn. "Lay off, will you?"

I reach for my phone inside my bag, turn it on, and stare at the blinking screen. Dad's left a ton of messages. I'm in so much trouble right now. I should just turn around and go back to the motel. Instead, I shove the phone deeper under the pile of notebooks, the blank pages I'll never finish, and a name that doesn't belong to me.

9

It's a house of glass. The walls are completely made of windows, but I can't see inside. Only the sky mirrored in the sloping panels of the roof. At first, I think it's some kind of art museum, then Shawn pulls into the driveway.

"This is your place?" I'm stunned.

"My dad's an architect," Shawn explains. "He came up with the design. It's his house, so why not go crazy? I mean, it's weird, right?"

I stare at the glass walls. "I think it's amazing."

And it is.

We get out of the car and start walking. I had no idea that Shawn lived in a place like this. In the distance, a boat dock leads to the water, framed by a row of palm trees draped in colorful beads.

"That's my mom's idea of a holiday decoration," he says, making his way through the jungle-like fronds. "It took forever, trying to hang all those beads. So we just left them there."

I lift my hand and touch the glittery strings. They're plastic, yet more beautiful than any Christmas tree I've ever seen. Does Shawn's family celebrate Christmas? I'm really curious, but I don't want to ask, in case I sound rude.

As we head inside, Shawn and his sister tug off their sneakers, so I unlace my Super Glue boots and plop them near the front door. I'm so embarrassed about the holes, but nobody seems to care. God, I can't remember the last time I walked around barefoot. It feels good. Real good, actually.

In the living room, a massive flat-screen TV floats on the wall like a painting. The couch is heaped with so many pillows, I could build a fort. Glass doors open onto a deck facing the bay, where a circle of wicker chairs surround a fire pit. I stand near the door, afraid to move in case I break something. I reach for my menthols, but smoking's probably not a good idea, so I shove my hands in my pockets.

"You want tea?" Shawn asks.

"Tea?"

"What? Did that sound funny?"

"No," I say quickly, hoping I didn't offend him. "I've never had a tea party before."

He laughs. "Well, let's get this party started."

I follow Shawn into the kitchen, shuffling my bare feet across those extra-soft rugs. The stove is so clean, I wonder if anyone cooks here. They probably cook once in a while because they've got two refrigerators, both stainless steel. All we have at the motel is a mini fridge crammed with microwave dinners.

Emily's already spooning milk into a gleaming saucepan. "Do you like chai?" she says as it starts to boil.

I'm not a big fan of tea, but this chai smells so amazing, I'll probably never drink Dad's insta-crack Bustelo again. Emily pours the tea through a strainer over a jade-green cup. Just holding it in my hands makes me feel extra glamorous.

"How is it?" she asks.

I take a big gulp. Not only does it taste good, but it makes me feel good too. "Best tea ever."

We stand in the kitchen, all three of us, sipping tea.

"Well, I have to go finish my research paper," she says, rinsing her cup in the sink.

"That sucks." I nod in sympathy.

"Tell me about it," she says. "The worst part is writing it all down. I mean, why can't I just talk about my brilliant observations?"

Shawn rolls his eyes. "You're going to be an awesome lawyer."

"Can't argue with that," she says, gliding upstairs.

I watch her disappear.

"Your sister's really cool," I tell him.

"That's what you think."

"For real. I wish I had a sister."

It's true. I always wanted a big sister. Someone to teach me things like how to twist my hair into French braids. Or how to ride a bike. I had to teach myself, falling over and over until the scabs crusted my knees.

Right now, I could really use a big sister. I used to tell Dad everything. He was my diary, always there to listen. Now we don't talk anymore. At least, not about stuff that actually matters.

Stuff like boys.

"So it's just you, huh? No sisters or brothers?" Shawn leans back against the counter and his foot bumps against mine. For a minute, I stay perfectly still, just so I don't break the connection.

"Yeah, it's just me. Guess my parents gave up after I came along."

"They got it right the first time."

A rush of heat tingles my neck. Is he flirting with me? I don't know what to do. I'm so used to being that girl. The quiet one. Invisible. I try to come up with a joke, but my mind goes blank. "Thanks for inviting me over."

"No problem. I'm glad you're here."

My face heats up again. "Your house is really nice, by the way." I glance around the kitchen. All those stainless steel gadgets. On the counter, Emily left one of her bracelets—a gold bangle studded with roses. It probably cost a lot. It would be easy, slipping it in my pocket. The thought jumps into my head so fast, it startles me.

Emily has so much.

She probably won't even notice it's gone.

"Hello?" a woman calls from the hallway. "What do I smell burning?"

"It's me," says Shawn. "I'm thinking too hard."

"Shawn Bryant, I told you not to use that copper saucepan," she says, marching into the kitchen. This must be Shawn's mom. She's even prettier than Emily, swishing around in loose-fitting black pants and a silky blouse.

He holds up his hands. "I'm innocent, I swear."

"Emily said you left it on the stove."

"Well, obviously she's lying. See what they're teaching her in law school?"

Mrs. Bryant turns around. "I'm sorry. I didn't see you standing there."

That's okay. I'm used to it.

"Reece, this is my mom," Shawn says, as if I haven't already figured it out.

She offers her hand. "Reece, is it?"

I can't help noticing her brightly painted nails, the way they shine. Her grip is soft, almost pillowy. I wonder if she's grossed out by the dirt caked under my thumbs.

"Are you a friend from school?" she asks.

A friend.

Is that what I am?

Before I can say anything, my phone goes off inside my bag. There's only one person on Earth who knows my cell number. Dad must be leaving another message. A crazy long message. How do I know? Because it starts ringing again.

"That's probably my dad," I say, but I still don't move.

Mrs. Bryant frowns. "You should call your father. I know how parents tend to worry."

Dad's not worried about me. He's just trying to control my life. At the same time, I feel a little guilty when the phone finally stops ringing.

"You're right. I'll call him back."

"Good girl." Mrs. Bryant gives me a hug, as if she's my mom too.

If only that were true.

Shawn pours more tea in my mug. "Drink up. Chai is like Iron Man's stealth armor."

"Thanks." I smile.

"I'll be in the living room, battling zombies on Minecraft." He gives me a salute, then follows his mom out of the kitchen.

When I take out my phone, the screen is blinking. Five new messages. Why won't he leave me alone? I turn it off and shove it in my bag. All of a sudden, I feel dizzy. I sit down at the table. The gold bracelet is right in front of me. I reach for it so fast, I don't have time to think.

"Are you okay?"

I spin around.

Emily marches into the kitchen. She yanks open a drawer and starts digging for something. "You seem a little out of it."

My heart is thudding like it's going to explode. As soon as that bracelet's in my pocket, I'm aching to put it back.

"I'm just tired," I tell her.

"I hear that. Honestly, I think this class in immigration law is my kryptonite. And my favorite pen just ran out of ink," she says, holding up a Sharpie. "Don't you hate when pens die for no reason?"

"They should come with an expiration date."

"Exactly." She sighs.

Why won't she leave?

Emily's still opening drawers, hunting for a pen. There's no way I can put the bracelet back without her seeing it.

"Good luck with your paper," I say, pushing back my chair. The gold bracelet is crammed deep in my pocket. I have to get rid of it. But how? I go into the living room, where Shawn's stretched out on the sofa, clutching a game controller, his gaze locked on the TV.

"Let me guess," he says. "Your dad's still freaking out?"

"My dad's always freaking out." I look at my bare feet and think about me and Dad salsa-dancing in the kitchen. I'm talking too much, but Shawn's listening. I don't expect him to understand. Why would he? Shawn's family is so normal. How am I supposed to explain that I've been hiding from the "bad guys" all my life?

I'm so tired of hiding.

I sit down next to him on the sofa. He clicks off the TV and puts his arm around my shoulder. My first instinct is to move away. Instead, I sink against his warmth. It feels good to just let go.

"This is my fault," he says quietly.

"No, it's not."

"Yeah, it is. For real. I should've brought you back to the motel. I didn't realize it was such a big deal."

"Everything's a big deal with my dad."

"What do you mean?"

I feel like I have to explain. "He's got no off switch. It's like he's constantly swinging from one extreme to the other."

"And your mom?" Shawn asks.

I shake my head.

"Sorry. My bad," he says. "That was totally out of bounds. I just thought... I don't know. Maybe if you talked to someone else. Then it wouldn't be all on you. Does that make sense?"

"It makes a lot of sense. And you don't have to apologize."

"Well, I'm apologizing anyway. I guess it's kind of weird that my parents are still together."

"I don't think it's weird."

"Yeah, well. All my friends' parents got divorced back when we were in middle school."

If only my mom and dad were divorced. Then it would be a hell of a lot easier to explain.

Shawn leans in closer. "Just hear me out, okay? I don't know what's going on with your mom. But your dad's problem with her...that doesn't have to be your problem. Maybe if you got on the phone with her—"

"That's not going to happen."

He winces. "Just trying to help."

I didn't mean to come off so harsh. God, I sounded exactly like Rage Dad. Maybe Shawn's right. I need to find out the truth about my mom.

"I'm sorry," I tell him. "You don't deserve to be yelled at."

He looks at me. "Yeah, that's something we can agree on."

"I should probably head back."

"Right." Shawn gets up and takes out his car keys. Actually, his sister's keys. "Let's hotwire the Tank."

The bracelet digs against my hip. I could shove it under the pillows and hope Emily finds it. That way, it will look like it fell off and landed there by itself. I slide a finger into my pocket, tracing the flowers sculpted into the metal.

"You coming or what?" Shawn's already tugging on his sneakers.

I lace up my boots and follow him outside. The guilt burns through me. Why did I have to sink so low? Shawn's family was really cool to me. Then I had to go and destroy everything.

We walk across the front lawn. The clouds are hanging low over the dock. A pelican dips across the bay, silently pumping its wings.

"Next time we'll take the boat out," Shawn tells me.

"Next time?"

He grins. "Unless you've got plans."

"So can you drive the boat somewhere? Or does it just… float around?" I feel stupid for asking.

"There's this amazing place in Crandon Park. You can only reach it by boat."

"You mean an island?"

"Something like that. How does Friday sound for you?"

"Sounds good."

If Dad doesn't kill me first.

We're almost at the driveway. I reach inside my pocket, tracing the shape of that gold bracelet. I need to get rid of it. Fast. I wait until Shawn's ahead of me. Then I fling that bracelet into the weeds.

"Hey, snake bite."

I spin around.

"You okay?" he asks.

"I'm mostly okay."

"For real? Because that's the name of my graphic novel. *I'm Mostly Okay: The Life of Shawn Bryant*."

"You actually made a graphic novel?"

"Maybe."

"I'm going to find it."

"Go ahead and try. I mean, if it actually exists. So let's start over. Are you okay? Because you seem a little stressed out."

The shame rises up. I can't even look at him.

"I just don't want to go home."

"In that case, should we take a walk?"

I nod.

Shawn grabs my hand and it feels right, as if it's meant to fit there. "Let's go. I've got a surprise for you."

The palms tilt and sway above us, their branches draped with beads. He's showing off a little, but I don't mind. Nobody's ever tried to impress me before. Maybe I am impressed. Not because Shawn lives in a big glass house with its own boat dock. Because he laughs at my stupid jokes. And he listens. Really listens, like we're the Earth's only survivors and even the lonely parrots have flown away.

10

The empty cages are hidden behind the pines. All the doors are flung wide open, the bars long gone, making it easy to sneak inside. No animals locked up here. Only the wild peacocks, dragging their tails in the dirt.

"Where are we?" I stare at the faded mural on the wall—seagulls swooping against a painted sky.

"My favorite hiding spot," says Shawn, following behind me. "This place used to be a zoo back in the day. It got trashed in a hurricane a long time ago."

Dirty rainwater speckles the concrete floor, along with things people left behind. Firecracker shells. Rusty beer cans. A feather so bright, it looks painted. I reach down and scoop up the feather. The blue-green swirls remind me of an eye keeping watch. "Thanks for showing me everything today."

"No problem," he says. "But you haven't seen everything yet."

"So when do I get to meet your dad?"

He looks away. "My dad's kind of old-school. Don't get me wrong. He's awesome. I just don't usually have friends at the house."

The f-word.

Friends.

"Do you understand?" he asks.

"Actually, I don't."

Maybe he's afraid of damaging my sensitive feelings or whatever. Well, screw it. I'd rather know the truth.

"Is it because I'm different?"

Shawn stays quiet.

"You're the first girl I've invited over," he finally says.

"Really?" I wasn't expecting that.

"Yeah, you're different. When I saw you marching across

the highway in those boots, I was like, who is this girl? You're different from anyone I've ever met. But that's not what you meant, is it?"

I don't know what to say.

I'm not rich like you.

He smiles. "Thanks for not judging me, Reece. You're pretty amazing. You know that?"

"Thanks," I say, lowering my head.

He's never called me that before. Not snake bite or some cheesy nickname. I trace my hand along the mural, as if I could dissolve into the sun-blistered paint. The faded blue sky is dotted with birds, all swarming across the horizon. It's what my art teacher would call rule of thirds. You line up everything until it's perfect, the way it never looks in real life.

"So what's your secret?" he asks.

"Secret?"

"I mean, when are you going to tell me?"

"Tell you what exactly?"

"Why are you living in a motel?"

I take a deep breath. Would it be easier if I told the truth? "Last summer, we got kicked out of our apartment." I'm trying to explain, but it comes out wrong. "My dad ran out of money and we couldn't pay rent. God, this is so embarrassing."

"There's something else going on," he says, looking at me. "Am I right?"

I stare at the puddles of rainwater on the floor. "Please don't make me answer that question."

"Are you in trouble?" Shawn grabs my hand. "Talk to me. No judgment, I swear."

"I'm sorry."

How can I explain?

My entire life is a lie.

"Now you're scaring me," he says.

I pull away from him. "Just leave me alone, okay?"

"Okay, snake bite. It's your call. But if you feel like talking, I'm here."

I want to talk to Shawn. God, I want it more than anything. The "bad guys" aren't coming after me.

I'm not a little kid anymore.

"Listen. I had a lot of fun with you today," I tell him.

"Me too," he says. "With you, I mean."

"So let's not mess it up."

He nods. "No more questions."

"Deal."

We don't say anything for a moment. Then Shawn brushes his lips against mine. He breathes into me and I'm safe. Nothing except his fingers tracing the curve of my back. The palm fronds rustling above us. A hint of salt water in the breeze, letting us know the ocean's nearby, even if I can't see it.

He gently lets go. "Wow. That was a surprise."

"Is that bad?"

"Surprises are good," he says, stroking my hair. "Especially that kind of surprise."

At that moment, I want to stay in his arms. Let the paint fade from the mural, the bars turn to rust, until all that's left are the peacock feathers, their silent eyes. When he kisses me again, the world goes quiet. Only the breeze rustling the fronds above us, and the faint song of a tree frog.

I turn my head.

"What's wrong?" he whispers.

I'm listening hard.

I've moved to dozens of cities. So many, I can't remember their names. There's only one place I can't forget. A place that comes to me in dreams. It's a feeling more than a memory.

Home.

છ

As we drive past the gas station, I scoot a little lower in my seat. This is the last place I want to be right now. The motel lights are a faint stain above the parking lot. It looks even skankier at night. An old man is slumped on a plastic chair, gnawing on chicken wings out of a Styrofoam carton. God, this is so embarrassing.

I lower my head between my knees.

"You doing okay?" Shawn asks.

"Just bracing myself for the inevitable meltdown."

"Well, if you need to talk, you've got my number, right?"

I take out my phone. "Text it to me?"

Before I get out of the car, he runs to the passenger side and opens the door for me. How cute is that? I'm kind of overwhelmed by his sweetness. To be honest, I don't feel like I deserve it.

"Thanks for rescuing me," I tell him.

"I'll rescue you anytime." He pulls me into a hug and I lean against his chest, breathing in his warmth. "Reece," he says, "you're shivering." He zips up my hoodie. For a second I think he's going to kiss me again. "Catch you tomorrow at school?"

Tomorrow.

My new favorite word.

I start walking toward the motel's neon sign. It stays on all night, yet never seems bright enough.

"Hey, snake bite," he calls out, coming toward me. "You forgot something." He holds up the peacock feather from the abandoned zoo.

Finders keepers.

In my mind, I see Emily's gold bracelet sparkling in the tall grass by the water. Maybe she's found it by now. At least, that's what I hope. God, why did I have to be so stupid?

I tuck the feather in my back pocket. "Sure you don't want it? Peacock feathers are supposed to be good luck."

"I don't need it," Shawn says, holding me close.

"Why not?"

"Because I'm the lucky one," he says and then he kisses me.

When I reach the motel room, I know something's not right. I shove my key in the door and it swings open, all by itself. Okay. That was weird. Did I leave the room unlocked? Maybe somebody's hiding in there, waiting for me. A bad man.

I click on the lights.

"Dad?" I whisper.

Silence.

The room is trashed. And I don't mean in a rock star sort of way. It just looks like shit. All the dresser drawers are yanked open. My T-shirts are crumpled on the floor. What the hell is going on? Dad's stretched out on the mattress in his boxers, staring into space.

"Where have you been?" he mumbles at me.

I wasn't gone that long. Is it really such a big deal? I mean, he's just lying there, practically butt naked. At least put on that stupid sweat suit. Jogging pants. Whatever they are.

I sit down on the edge of the bed. "Sorry I didn't call back."

Here's the saddest part. I want to tell Dad what happened today. The palm trees decorated with Christmas beads. The abandoned zoo on Key Biscayne.

I used to tell Dad everything. He didn't even get mad when I punched Dave Gursky in the stomach back in middle school. Trust me. That kid deserved it. He kept following me through the lunch room, yelling stuff like, "What's wrong with your face?" Yeah, that's totally original.

Dad showed me the proper way to throw a punch. You have to tuck your thumb outside your fist. Otherwise you'll smash your bones.

"You should've knocked that kid's teeth out," he told me.

Now he's the one I want to beat up.

He stretches out his hand. "Give me your phone."

"What?"

"Your phone. Is it broken?"

I shake my head.

Dad frowns. "Give it to me."

When I don't move, he gets out of bed. It takes me a second to realize what's going on. He's digging inside my Hail Kale bag, throwing stuff all over the floor. He pulls out my phone.

"Who's Shawn?" he asks.

"Just some guy from school."

That's what comes out of my mouth.

"Is he your boyfriend?"

"I don't know."

I feel so stupid, answering Dad's perverted questions.

"What do you mean, 'I don't know'?" he says, raising his voice. "Is this guy your boyfriend or not?"

"I don't know, okay?"

"You're fooling around with this…Shawn. And you don't know if he's your boyfriend?"

Wait. Dad thinks I'm having sex? This is beyond embarrassing. Not to mention, a thousand miles from reality.

"Get off my phone."

I reach for it, but Dad's still clicking away, going through my messages. He lifts his head. "This is my house. And in my house there are rules."

What a freaking joke, Dad. This isn't your house.

It's nobody's.

"I'm sick of your stupid rules."

"Yeah?" he says. "My rules are what's keeping us safe."

"Safe from what? I mean, come on."

Dad marches over to the door and yanks it open. At first I think he's going to run outside. He does that sometimes. Takes off. He swings back his arm and tosses my phone into the parking lot.

"Why did you have to break it?" I'm shouting at him. "I hate you."

He flinches. "Don't say that. It isn't true."

At that moment, it is true. I hate my dad more than any living, breathing human on the planet. And I want him to feel every sliver of pain he's scraped into me. All the unfixable damage.

"I wish you left me with Mom."

He sinks down onto the mattress and sort of droops, as if all his strings have been pulled out. "You're just like her. Stubborn as hell."

Wait.

What did he say?

How can I be like someone if they're dead?

Yeah, Dad's told me a hundred times. He's the only one I can trust. At least, it's what he taught me to believe, ever since I was a little kid. He taught me lots of things, like how to steal without getting caught. And how to lie.

"There was a cop at school today."

Dad widens his eyes. Now he's paying attention. "You sure that was a cop?"

"I'm sure."

There's no doubt in my mind. That guy at school was watching me. I remember the way he leaned against the chain-link fence, scanning the field with his laser stare. The beaded chain tucked inside his shirt. The plain white tee. Yeah, he was a cop. I could tell just by looking at him.

Dad's pacing back and forth, stepping over piles of boxes and garbage bags on the floor. "Did you mess up?"

"I didn't do anything."

"What makes you think he's after you?"

I can't explain. Call it a hunch. A gut instinct. Whatever. Now I've got to decide. Do I trust this feeling? Or pretend it's not whispering in the back of my mind, daring me to listen?

"He's watching me, Dad. I think he knows who I am."

"Listen up, needle legs," he says. "And you better listen good. If that was a cop, we're packing everything in the van. You hear me?"

The thought of moving again makes me sick. I don't want to live in the backseat of a van with my dad. I want my own space. A normal life. Friends.

I want to go home.

Meanwhile, Rage Dad is back in full force. "You must've done something wrong," he says, glaring. "Tell the truth."

The truth?

I don't even know what that is.

"Now it's your turn," I say.

He stares at the floor. "I don't know what you're talking

about."

"Is my mom still alive?"

The silence hangs between us. I wait for Dad to start lying again. Instead, he doesn't say anything. That's all I need to hear.

I grab the keys off the table and shove past him into the breezeway. Then I run like hell. I don't look back. I just keep running. I pound down the stairs and head straight for the parking lot. My phone's got to be around here somewhere. What's left of it. Finally, I spot a mangled lump of plastic on the ground. I crouch down and scoop up the broken pieces.

"Get back here. Now," Dad hollers, sprinting down the steps.

His van is parked at the edge of the lot. That way, he can keep an eye on it from the motel room. I make a run for it. Dad's right behind me, but I've got a head start. I shove the key in the door and pull it open. As I climb in the backseat, he's screaming at full volume. I'm sure the entire motel can hear it. Not that anybody cares. In this place, we've all got our own problems.

I hit the lock.

Dad bangs his fist on the window. "You hear me?"

I scoot down lower. The floor is a wasteland of crumpled fast food wrappers and plastic bottles. This is probably what the bottom of the ocean will look like in a million years.

When he's finally gone, I take out my phone, but I can't get it to turn on. I think about Shawn, our kiss. His fingers tracing my back. The soft warmth of his mouth on mine.

Nobody's ever kissed me before.

I used to imagine it would be like those romance books I dig out of the garbage. It was different with Shawn. He made me feel special. And his family was so nice to me. Why did I have to destroy everything?

Shawn's right. I need to find out the truth about Mom.

Is it possible that she's still alive?

I don't believe in the "bad guys" anymore. There's something else I have to consider. Something that scares me more than any red-eyed monster hiding in the trees.

What if Dad's the bad guy?

The halo of a flashlight cuts across the parking lot. I sit up and peer through the windshield. The old men are playing dominoes under the street lamp. Their arms move back and forth over the table, sweeping up the pieces, all those dots that add up to nothing.

I lean back against the seat and close my eyes. I can't let Shawn know the truth. I'm not the girl he thinks I am.

I really wish I was.

11

If you can get her to start, she's yours." The old guy stood on his porch, watching Dad brush pine needles off the van. The field behind the trailer was a graveyard of cars rusting into the dirt. As soon as Dad saw the van, he offered a fistful of cash, right there on the spot. We'd been "camping" in the woods for days. I guess he knew that couldn't last.

The trailer looked like it was about to cave-in. The roof was thick with tree branches and all the windows were Xed out with masking tape. While Dad messed around under the hood, I shoved handfuls of grass to the rabbits in this wire cage on the porch. The old guy pulled one out by the ears—a small, pink-eyed clump of fur that wouldn't stop squirming.

"What's his name?" I asked.

The old guy clenched the cigarette between his teeth. "Dinner."

I started crying and freaking out. Now I was in big trouble. Dad said I wasn't supposed to cry. Ever. I had to be tough like a boy. When he came back, he asked, "What happened?" but I didn't say anything.

We got in the van and drove away. I watched the porch grow small in the rearview mirror.

"Was that man a bad guy?" I whispered.

Dad steered down a winding dirt road. I had no idea where we were going. It felt like we'd been hiding in the woods forever. After a while, he said, "Maybe a little good and bad."

How could you be both?

I kept thinking about the rabbits. "Why are they in a cage?" I asked over and over, hoping he'd say something to take the hurt away.

"Keeps them safe," he said.

"Safe from what?"

He thought for a minute.

"Snakes."

That's what he told me.

I stared out the window at the trees. "Can we go home now?"

"What did I tell you? Don't ask me again."

"But I want to see Mommy."

He jerked the steering wheel and we swerved off the road. Dad cut the ignition and for a long time we sat in the van, not going anywhere.

"Your mother's dead," he snapped.

I kicked my feet against the windshield. Screamed until my throat burned. Pounded my fists on the glass. Still, it didn't break.

When I finally slumped forward, Dad threw his arms around me. "It's going to be okay," he said, but I didn't believe him.

Dad cranked up the radio. He knew all the words to "You Never Can Tell."

"C'est la vie," he said, thumping the steering wheel.

"What does that mean?"

He winked. "It's the language of love."

For a moment, we didn't say anything.

"Did you love Mom?"

It just popped out.

He kept his gaze on the road. "I did."

"But now you don't."

"You're my love," he said.

That's not the same thing.

"Listen up, needle legs." Dad always smiled when he called me that. He wasn't smiling anymore. His voice did that changey thing. That's how I knew I was in trouble. "What happened today was really dangerous."

I squeezed my fingers open and closed.

"You talked to a stranger."

Open. Closed.

"How many strangers can you talk to?"

"None," I whispered.

"Say it again."

"I can't talk to anybody."

"Do you know why?" he asked.

"Yeah."

"Tell me."

"Because I'm a girl."

Dad got this strange look on his face. "It's not about being a girl. Okay? I don't want you feeling ashamed of that."

Why would I feel ashamed?

"It's just easier." He stared at the power lines rising in the distance. "When we get our new place, you can be a girl again."

"Promise?"

Dad stroked my hand. "I promise."

"Pinky promise?"

"Pinky promise," he said, hooking his finger around mine. "I love you, needle legs. You know that, right?"

"How much?"

"More than sunshine," he said.

"And dinosaurs?"

"A lot more than dinosaurs."

"And mermaids?"

"I love you more than mermaids," he said, looking at me. "More than all the fishes in the ocean."

That night, it stormed so bad, we pulled off the highway. The van smelled like wet dog, but it was better than sleeping in a tent. We stretched out in the backseat with our feet pressed against the window.

"Look at your toes," Dad said, pointing at my feet. "Your second one's bigger than your first."

"So?"

"That means you're really smart. You're going to be something special," he told me. "Don't turn into a no good bum like your dad."

Weeks later, it was still raining. Dad drove for miles, zooming down highways and country roads. I had no idea where we were going. Everything that was mine was gone. I tried to remember the sound of Mom's voice. I saw her body crumpled on the floor, her face tipped away from me. The bad guys hurt her. If I wasn't good, they would hurt me too.

Dad didn't look like himself anymore. A beard etched his jaw and a wing of thick dark hair curled over his forehead. I must've looked different too. I could pull off my jeans without unbuttoning them. We stole food out of dumpsters. Sometimes we didn't eat for days. I learned to live with the dull, throbbing ache in my belly. It was part of me now and it wasn't going away.

Sometimes Dad was in a good mood. Sometimes he wasn't. We played Highway Bingo and Raindrop Races. I'd count the drops squiggling down the window, searching for the one that belonged to me.

I spy with my little eye...

Dad pointed at things hidden beside the road. Horses grazing in a field. A red barn on top of a hill. The bones of a fence that collapsed long ago.

"Did you see?" he asked.

I looked, but couldn't find it.

He kissed my cheek. "It doesn't matter who wins."

That's because he always did.

12

Somebody's tapping on the window. I sit up straight, as if I'm about to levitate out of the van. Sunlight dribbles across the backseat. It takes me a second to remember where I am. The epic fight with Dad. My smashed-up phone.

Tappity, tap, tap.

A face pops up behind the windshield. Frizzy hair stapled with curlers. Earrings the size of cereal nuggets.

"You okay?" Fruit Loop shouts.

Obviously, I'm doing great.

She bangs her fist against the glass.

"Open," she says.

You can't actually "open" a car, but I know what she means. Fruit Loop's still going off, so I unlock the van and get out. Then I see a pair of dark brown eyes blinking up at me.

"Why are you sleeping in there?" Mouse wants to know.

I can't believe it.

She talked.

Actually, I didn't know she could talk at all.

"It's my secret hideout," I tell her.

Mouse nods, as if she knew all along. "I'm good at hiding."

Fruit Loop gets this weird look on her face. "Be quiet," she tells Mouse, then turns to me. "You in trouble?"

That's sort of an understatement.

"My dad's kind of pissed."

I should watch the four-letter words around Mouse, but she's probably heard worse.

Fruit Loop sighs. "Come with me. First you eat. Then we talk."

Talk? I'm not talking to this crazy old lady. That's for sure.

As we march upstairs, I keep glancing over my shoulder, half-expecting Dad to show up. I really hope he doesn't. Still,

I'm kind of worried about him. How stupid is that? Dad's supposed to be taking care of me. Not the other way around.

Fruit Loop's place is next door, but it might as well be the surface of Mars. I follow Mouse inside the cramped motel room. The floor is a minefield of sleeping bags and kiddie junk. I step over a toy lawnmower filled with plastic beads. Wow. How stupid is this thing? It's like, here you go, little girl. Dream big.

All of a sudden, a dog comes galloping out of nowhere. And I don't mean the fluffy, ankle-biting variety. I'm talking a full-grown beast. He might even have a little pit in him. Who knows? He sinks next to me, thumping his tail.

Fruit Loop drags out a chair. "Sit."

I sit.

Kids and dogs. This lady's broke as hell, yet she's feeding everything with a pulse in this motel. Pets are totally off-limits, but that didn't stop her from sneaking the mutt into her room. I have to admit, she's got balls of steel. Dad won't let me get a dog, no matter how many times I begged.

"You hungry?" She's messing with a coffee maker, crumbling a packet of ramen noodles where you're supposed to pour hot water. Actually, that's kind of genius. If you're living in a motel, it's all about making things up as you go.

When we were sleeping in the van, Dad used to wrap hamburger meat in tinfoil and sizzle it on the engine. Or he'd plug a crock-pot into the cigarette lighter and dump a can of stew into it. We chowed down on all kinds of good stuff—Beef-a-roni, mac 'n' cheese, Sloppy Joes, you name it.

Wait. Is it lunchtime already?

I've racked up a gazillion LDs for missing class. I never turned in my stupid research paper. Now I'm going to be kicked out of school.

"I have to go," I tell her, scraping back my chair.

She pushes me back down. "Sit."

I don't have time to sit.

Mouse blinks at me. "Please?"

I sit.

Together we eat in the motel room, slurping ramen noodles from giant mugs. No spoons. That's kind of appropriate, considering Mouse's grandma heated this stuff with Mr. Coffee. I mean, the old lady's got to be her grandmother, right?

I glance up at Fruit Loop. If she's a grandmother, she definitely falls in the youngish category. Her face is tired, but her neck isn't floppy and birdlike. At least, not yet. She catches me staring and I look away.

"Thanks for lunch," I tell her. "This is probably the best thing I've eaten in a million years."

"Dirty cooking." She laughs.

Mouse tilts back her head, guzzling every last drop of instant ramen. She's so blissed out, it almost makes me sick. Why is she so happy? We're trapped inside this prison, all of us, and there's no escape.

"You live here with your dad?" she asks.

"Something like that."

"We just got here," Mouse says, as if I didn't know. "Me and my mom, we used to…" she stammers, taking another gulp. "We used to be at New Life."

I'm guessing that's a homeless shelter.

"Where's your mom now?"

Mouse shrugs.

God, I should learn to keep my mouth shut.

She licks her spoon. "When we move out, I'm getting a fish tank. And lots of angel fishes."

"That's cool. I used to have a fish tank."

"Really?" She smiles.

I need to get out of here, but it's kind of nice, talking to someone. Mouse is the only friend I've got in this place.

The dog stretches out his legs and rests his head on my feet, as if I'm part of the family now. He whines a little and flicks his ears, as if he's dreaming. I didn't even realize dogs could dream.

"We found him in a box," Mouse tells me.

"A box?"

"He had a rope around his neck and he was going like this."
She sticks out her tongue.

So her dog's a sky rat too.

We all are.

When I'm finished, Mouse hands me a piece of Gummi
candy. Probably from the same bag I gave to her. God, that
already seems like forever ago. I rub my eyes. Still, the tears leak
out.

Fruit Loop puts her mug on the floor. Then she rushes over
to me. She crouches down and pushes back my hair, stroking
my forehead.

I let her.

"Lord," she says, tugging at my bandana. "Girl, what happened to you?" Her thumb moves across my forehead, tracing
it like a map. I'm so tired, I don't even care. Go ahead. Take a
good look at the freak. It's like she's seeing me for the first time,
her eyes leaking through me.

She knows.

This woman knows who I am.

I pull away from her grip. She's spitting out words I can't
understand. Only broken pieces rise to the surface.

"The little girl," she says. "You were missing."

I'm not a little girl.

Don't tell me that I'm missing.

How can I be missing if nobody tried to find me?

I run inside the bathroom and punch the lock. You could
say I've had a lot of practice in that department, but I can't stay
trapped inside the bathroom forever. Fruit Loop's pounding on
the door.

"Open," she hollers.

I squint at the rectangle of sunlight over my head. The window's way too high for me. If I stand on the edge of the tub, I
can almost reach it. Almost.

The genetic lottery strikes again.

Above the tub, there's a square-shaped ledge cut into the

tiles. You're supposed to put soap in there, but it's empty. I shove my foot into that narrow space, reach up and cling to the windowsill. Now I can see the breezeway. All the moth-plastered light bulbs, the air conditioners roaring in their cages. If I can squeeze through that window, I'm free.

Fruit Loop rattles the doorknob. She's making so much noise, I wouldn't be surprised if Booth showed up. I glance around the bathroom. The shower rod is bolted to the wall. Can't reach it anyway. Come on, Reece. Use your head.

I step onto the soap ledge. Reach up and grab the plastic wand dangling next to the blinds. When I give it a tug, it droops an inch. Another tug and it's halfway down the wall. One more and the blinds go crashing down.

By now, Fruit Loop's probably figured out what I'm doing. It doesn't matter. I got what I needed. The plastic wand isn't very sturdy, but it will have to do. I pop it off the blinds and I'm good to go.

That window hasn't been opened in a while. What if it's stuck? I jab the wand against the latch and give it a push. The dusty pane tilts up like a trapdoor. Can I squeeze through it? Only one way to find out. I slide my leg over the windowsill. My pulse thumps in my fingers and toes and all the empty spaces between. Every piece of me throbbing with fear.

I push myself over and jump.

13

Dad's van is parked in its usual spot, the windshield crusted with bird shit. By the time I reach it, I'm out of breath. This is insane. I've never driven a car before. It can't be too hard, right? I don't have a license. Not even a learner's permit. If a cop pulls me over, I'm screwed.

When I slide behind the wheel, it feels so strange. The tank's almost empty. Just enough to get to school, if I don't kill myself. I click on the seatbelt and pray I don't crash. The engine revs up. No problem. Okay. I got this.

I swerve out of the parking lot. The van's shaking like it's going to explode. Dad says the shocks are fried. At least that's what he thinks. God, he's going to kill me. Maybe he won't notice it's gone? Yeah, right.

The windshield's so dirty, I can barely see where I'm going. I'm way up high above the traffic. Actually, this is kind of nice. Now I'm zooming down Eighth Street like a boss. I speed past the bus stop, where a bunch of old ladies are hunched on the bench, fanning themselves with newspapers.

I keep going past the Farmacias and Pain Clinics with the rusty cages bolted to the doors. A truck swings in front of me, blasting its horn. There's a bunch of guys hanging in the back, making kissy faces at me.

I'm so freaked out, I roll straight through a red light. I crank down the window and peer out, half-expecting a swarm of cops to pull up, but I'm good. I dip my fingers in the breeze and gulp the longest breath of my life.

For once, I'm in the driver's seat.

❧

I'm sweating like crazy by the time I reach the D.A.R.E. fence with the red plastic cups. The school parking lot's off-limits. I don't have a tag or whatever, so I cruise into a space marked VISITOR and hope I don't get towed.

No sign of Mr. Plain White Tee, but as I hustle toward the front office, the security guard rumbles by on a golf cart. I flash my student ID and he nods. Guess he's got more important things to do. No wonder the school voted to install metal detectors.

I push through the double doors and bust into the office. For some reason, it smells like burnt popcorn. Ms. Vitelli is slouched at her desk, pushing buttons on an ancient computer. She always wears a pin on her baggy sweatshirts. Today it's a giant strawberry.

"Reece Avery?" she says, like my name is a question. "Where are you supposed to be?"

I stare at the poster framed on the wall. Kittens dangling off a tree branch. Hang in there! My brain isn't functioning right now. I don't have my backpack. I don't even have a pen.

Where am I supposed to be?

"Um. It's second period, right?"

Ms. Vitelli takes off her glasses, as if she's tired of looking at me. "For ten more minutes."

"I'm supposed to be in bio, I think?"

She sighs. "Doesn't sound like you're thinking much at all."

Why is she judging me? I'm so pissed off, I want to shove that computer off her desk. Wipe the files clean. All the final grades and missed classes.

Ms. Vitelli's going off about my permanent record. Does she actually think I care? If I'm late for bio, my cells aren't going to stop dividing. At least, not anytime soon. My toenails will keep growing after I'm dead.

There is no permanent record.

"I'm missing a quiz. Can you please give me a late pass?" I ask her.

I can't remember what I'm supposed to study for that stupid bio quiz. Most of the time, I'm so bored in class, I flip ahead and read the next chapter. Then the next. If only things worked that way in real life.

Okay, I lied. There's one thing I remember. Every cell in my body has its own built-in expiration date. The whole circle of life thing. If that's true, it means you're always changing. You're never the same person.

"This is your third unexcused tardy," she says, pounding on that clunky old desktop. You'd think the school would've updated those prehistoric computers by now. They probably ran out of money after sodding the field with new grass for the baseball players to spit on.

"What do you mean, 'third unexcused tardy'?" God, I really hate that word tardy. In my head, it always sounds like turd.

"Three," she repeats, like I didn't hear the first time, "which counts as one unexcused absence."

I'm pretty good at math. I know three doesn't add up to one. This is so wrong. Not to mention, impossible.

"How many absences do I have so far?"

She squints at the computer. "This is your fifth."

"But I'm standing right here!"

"I'm sorry," she says, which is a complete lie. "School policy."

"What's school policy?"

"After five unexcused absences, we need to make a decision."

"A decision about what?"

"Your parents might have to go to truancy court."

Dad has to go to court because I missed class? This is bad. Really bad. Is she going to call child protective services? What if Dad goes to jail? It makes no freaking sense. If my dad gets locked up, how's that going to keep me in school?

I'm seriously about to lose it. When the baseball gods miss class, they're smoking near the Ditch. I'm not a baseball god. And I didn't miss class because I was hanging out by a drainage canal, smothering my lungs with nicotine. I'm too busy doing other things. Jumping out of motel windows, for example.

"Please." I'm begging her. "Just give me a late pass."

Ms. Vitelli frowns. "I'll sign you in," she says like it's a big favor. "But I want to make sure you understand. This isn't going away."

Of course it's not.

I grab the stupid paper and bolt toward the door.

"Reece?"

Now what? I've already racked up enough humiliation for one day.

She wipes her glasses on her sleeve. "I'll be sending a letter to your home."

Go ahead and send it. You'll be wasting trees because my dad's not going to read that letter. When he finds out that Fruit Loop knows who I am, it's game over. We'll be packing our bags and speeding to the next town.

I'm not going to let that happen.

Here's the deal. I still don't get how she recognized me. Yeah, my Stain gave me away. Did I show up on the news a long time ago? My head is full of questions I can't answer.

Forget class. The library is where I need to be. I push through the hall and slam past a bunch of sophomores in full-on pajamas. The school tried to ban them from wearing PJs because it's "too distracting." Obviously, they didn't listen.

A boy with a crew cut shoves his way in front of me. He's in my bio class, but I'm never there, which is probably why I can't remember his name.

"Hey," he says. "Didn't you wear that outfit yesterday?"

"No, you're hallucinating." I figure this will shut him up.

He smirks. "Then why do you reek so bad?"

My eyes are burning. I head straight for the girls' bathroom and duck inside the nearest stall. Does it matter if I'm wearing the same dirty Walmart jeans? I mean, does anyone really care?

I've spent a lot of time crying in bathrooms. Especially when me and Dad were living in the van. The nearest gas station was the only place where I could do normal stuff. Brush my teeth. Take a shower. Or a "bird bath" as Dad called it. He tried to act like this was okay. Maybe even fun.

It wasn't fun.

When it's finally quiet, I come out and bend over the sink, bird bath-style, and rinse off my sweat. Not much of an improvement. Better than walking around the school smelling like ass. I lift my T-shirt and start splashing. Don't even think about touching that nasty pink soap. I've seen people spit in it. How gross is that? I'm saying all these prayers inside my head, making deals with the Big Guy upstairs.

God, I'm sorry we don't talk much (not that you talk to me, either). But can you do one thing? Please help me find Mom. I promise I won't steal stuff anymore. I'll be good, I swear.

Is she still alive?

The library's front door is criss-crossed with bright yellow tape, as if somebody got murdered in there. I guess it's supposed to be a homecoming decoration. The window is swarming with magic marker: YOLO! How stupid is that? Yeah, you only live once, but the same is true for dying.

I duck under the tape and sneak inside. I really should be in class right now, but Ms. Kent always lets me hide in the so-called study room. Not that anyone ever studies in those bean-bag chairs.

The sharp tang of moldy carpet burns my throat as I move past the shelves. Buckets are scattered around the room, catching drips from the ceiling. Above the staircase, thin strips of insulation dangle like birthday streamers.

"Don't go up there."

I turn around.

Ms. Kent is marching past the empty tables. You'd think she'd be in a good mood all the time. I mean, she's surrounded by books. For some reason, she's always pissed off at the world. Maybe because she never gets to read anything.

"The roof's leaking," she tells me.

"I just need to use a computer," I mumble.

"I'm sorry. The computer lab is closed right now."

"It's for my research paper." Don't ask why I needed to throw in that lie. I guess I'm just used to lying all the time.

She reaches up and yanks the clip out of her hair, which is threaded with bright turquoise streaks. Ms. Kent is actually kind of young. I heard she used to go to this school. Why she came back here, I'll never know.

"Aren't you supposed to be in class?" she says.

I reach inside my Hail Kale bag and take out the late pass. "I've got independent study."

Ms. Kent barely glances at it. "Okay, Reece. Follow me."

Instead of going upstairs, we walk to a corner of the library where a bunch of PCs are lined up on a table. A clump of random boys are watching skate videos on YouTube. All seniors, of course. Looks like I'm not the only one on independent study.

"You've got twenty minutes," says Ms. Kent, walking away.

I was hoping for a little more privacy, but I don't have a choice. I squeeze between the boys and pull out a chair. A boy looks back at me and rolls his eyes, as if I did something wrong just by breathing the same air.

When I get online, the first thing I see is the school's website. Home of the fighting conchs. It's kind of weird that our mascot is basically something you'd order at a seafood restaurant (if you asked me, they should've picked a wooly mammoth). I'm taking a big risk. There's no way I should be doing this at school, but I'm running out of time. I click over to Google and type: MISSING GIRL, and next to it, my name.

The screen fills with girls. Little girls with spaces between their teeth. Not-so-little girls holding hands with their boyfriends. Girls standing in a crowd of blurred faces, as if everybody else doesn't exist.

This isn't the first time I've searched for myself online. It's kind of impossible when you don't have a computer. Not to mention, Dad's always watching me. Once in a while, I'll think, *Today's the day.* I'll scroll through the pictures in the news. I'll look at the smiling faces of those little girls. Could one of them be me?

They were walking home from school. Or a party. They got a ride in a friend's car and disappeared forever. This one girl? She was sleeping in her bed, safe and warm. The next morning, she was gone.

How many girls were kidnapped by their own dad?

For some reason, I'm pissed at those missing girls. They're taking up the space where I should be. I know it sounds weird, but I can't help it. I stare at the computer, searching for answers. Why isn't my face in the news? Maybe it's been too long. Too many years have passed. Or maybe I'm not looking in the right place.

My fingers shake as I type MIAMI into the search box. The pictures change again. I keep scrolling through pages, looking for clues. The first thing I see is a picture from the *Miami Herald*—a little girl in a lacy white dress, laughing on a swing.

There are things in the picture I can't see. The swing's been there so long, the rope has melted into the bark. At night the frogs sing. I squint at the little girl in that photo. I can't see her luna moth wings. They're lost in the shadow above her eye, a stain from the past.

That little girl is me.

Did my mom take that picture? Or was it Dad? You'd think a missing kid would be front page stuff, but it's under local news. I scroll down. Then I read the words that turn my blood to ice.

PRESUMED DEAD

Under the headline, there's a photo of a woman. She's looking off into the distance, her face damp with tears. I study her mouth, the space above her lip where the angels kissed her in the clouds.

Mom.

I can barely read the caption below that picture. "The bodies of the suspect and his daughter have not been recovered." It goes on and on. Something about a truck sinking into a canal off the Florida Turnpike.

My mom isn't dead.

I am.

All this time, I've been dead. I remember that first night. Dad sneaking off into the woods. His jeans soaking wet, as if he'd gone for a swim. When the cops dragged his truck out of the canal, they couldn't find my body. Still, they'd rather give up than admit they failed.

Dad killed off the missing part of me. He took away my past and invented a new person, a little boy named Reece. I think of the cold edge of his pocketknife against my neck. The trailer where he brought the van back to life. The rabbits in that cage, their pink eyes and crooked teeth.

The newspaper says Mom filed a police report after Dad took off. It says my disappearance has stunned the community of South Florida. It says my parents are "nomads" who fled south, hoping for a better life.

My mom is a sky rat too?

All this time, I only knew Dad's version of the truth. He hid my mom from it, erasing her from the picture.

I scan through the article again. At first, I'm not sure if I got it right. The newspaper says Dad was in some kind of trouble up north. He stole a bunch of money and was supposed to go to jail.

Before I can scroll down, someone taps my shoulder. A boy in a denim jacket is standing behind my chair, giving me a dirty look.

"Are you using that computer?" he asks.

I nod.

"Doesn't look like it," he says, huffing away.

I've been staring at this computer screen for so long, my eyes are bleary. How could Dad keep this a secret from me? Now I have something I didn't before.

My parents' names.

I do a quick search online, but I don't get very far. Whatever happened to Dad is buried now. A stain from the past. I try

searching for Mom and find a dog-walker in Queens. A DJ in
Atlanta. Hundreds of faces I don't recognize.

There's one thing I haven't tried yet. Dad won't let me have
Facebook or anything like that, but it doesn't take long to set up
an account. When I'm finished, I go back and type Mom's name
into the search box.

The screen fills with profiles. Too many people. There's a girl
in a tank top and skinny jeans, smiling into a bathroom mirror.
A girl who loves horses. A profile with no picture at all. Just a
box with the outline of a nameless head.

I scroll down to the bottom of the page. There's a woman
with a small, wiry-haired puppy snuggled on her lap. She isn't
smiling. In fact, she looks kind of sad. She's got tiny feet like
mine. Bare shoulders. Hair so long, it falls like a shadow over
her throat.

This woman is my mom.

Not the sad-eyed Mom I saw in the newspaper. She's older
now, but I recognize the way she's tilting her face, as if listening
to music inside her head.

I scroll down and a video starts playing at full volume.

Heads turn. Everybody's staring at me. God, I can't get this
thing to turn off. Ms. Kent rushes over to my computer and
presses a button on the keyboard.

"You've got five minutes left," she says, passing me a set of
headphones.

"Thanks," I whisper.

I'm almost afraid to watch the video posted on her page.
Who knows what I'm going to find? Maybe the truth. Whatever
that is.

I slide on the headphones and click PLAY.

A grey-haired man in a suit and tie walks across an empty
stage. He's all alone in a puddle of spotlight, looking straight at
the camera.

"On that night, a family was broken forever," he says, frowning into the camera as if this means a lot to him.

The video fades to black.

Now we're in a little girl's bedroom. On her dresser, the blue light of a fish tank throws shadows on the wall. She's asleep when a tall, stern-faced man comes into her room. He carries her in his arms like a princess in a fairy tale.

That little girl is supposed to be me.

It's so ultra-dramatic, I almost feel like laughing. I watch Fake Dad shove his daughter into the truck and speed away.

What happened before they left the house? The video doesn't show my mom and dad fighting. It doesn't show Mom crumpled on the floor, her hair spread out like the Virgin Mary's halo.

I still don't have the answer.

"Let's bring this little girl home," says the man in the suit.

I go back to the beginning and watch it again. Dad shoving me in the truck in the middle of the night. The actress who isn't me. The cheesy music thudding in the background, drums pounding like crazy.

I watch it again.

And again.

"Where is she now?" a voice booms through the darkness.

For a second, I think the show's over, but the music starts playing again. We're floating through a hallway. It reminds me of the way people talk about death. A light at the end of a tunnel.

The walls are lined with endless rows of lockers. All of a sudden, a crowd spills into the hallway—kids with big white teeth and fancy messenger bags, as if it's a back-to-school commercial.

A girl steps in front of the camera and opens her locker. All her books are neatly stacked and there's a mirror glued to the door. She's got amazing organizational skills. I give her that much. When she turns around, my stomach clenches. Above her left eyebrow, a stain. Her luna moth wings. A make-up artist probably brushed it on for the TV show.

A number flashes above a computer-generated photo. The face in that picture doesn't really look like me. Or maybe it could look like me, if Dad hadn't bleached my hair and pierced my lip. Still, I can't help wondering how many people have already called that number on the screen.

My hands are shaking so bad, I grip the edge of my chair. I keep looking at that girl on the TV. The make-believe me. How is this even possible? Maybe it was just a matter of time before Dad got busted.

Mom posted this video on her Facebook page a couple weeks ago. It's so weird to think that millions of people have watched it by now. A million strangers judging me and Dad. It doesn't matter where I hide. Somebody's going to recognize me. God, this is so messed up. I didn't want things to happen this way. This was supposed to be about my family. Not the entire world.

"Ten years have passed since she disappeared," says the dude in the suit, blinking into space. "Over a dozen witnesses have recently come forward, claiming to have seen the girl in South Florida. And for this reason, her mother refuses to give up hope."

The video fades to black.

It's over.

I stare at Mom's Facebook profile. This is the woman who held me as a baby, yet I know absolutely nothing about her. At the top of the page, there's a box that says, MESSAGE. I click on it and another box pops up. What am I supposed to say? *Hey, remember me? I'm your daughter who vanished ten years ago!*

The boys next to me are laughing at something on You-Tube—a dog riding a skateboard. I glance back at my computer. The blinking cursor. Mom's face. Her lipsticked mouth clenched tight. What can I say to make her trust me? Dear Mom doesn't sound right. She hasn't been my mom since I was a little kid.

I go with Mom and hope that's okay.

Dad said you were a ghost.
I want to know the truth.

I'm here in Miami.
Can we meet?

My finger hovers over the keyboard.
I hit SEND

The rest of the day passes in a haze. It's like I'm watching myself on that TV show about missing girls all over again. Over a dozen witnesses have seen me. Or think they've seen me. Is that why Mr. Plain White Tee showed up at school? Who tipped him off? Maybe someone at the motel. People come and go so quickly in that place, it's impossible to keep track. Anyway, I don't care who ratted me out. All that matters is that my mom is alive. Now there's only one thing left to do:

I've got to find her before the cops find me.

Class is finally over. Not that I spent much time in class. On my way out, I swing by the library again, but all the computers are taken. I'll have to wait until tomorrow to check if Mom answered my Facebook message. I've waited a decade. I can wait a little bit longer.

Right now, I've got another problem. The van's been parked in the visitor lot at school all day. I glance across the rows of cars. No sign of Mr. Plain White Tee. Still, I can't shake the feeling that he's out there, watching.

Shawn isn't here, either. He probably thinks I'm shutting him out. That's what sucks so bad. My phone is smashed to pieces. I never had a chance to read his texts. I really hope he gives me a chance to explain. He has no clue what's going on in my life.

There's a part of me that wants to run like hell. Go to the police and say, *Here's your missing girl.* Still, I can't do that to Dad. He's always been there for me, despite the bad stuff he's done in the past.

I need to keep him safe.

When I pull up to the motel, Dad's parking spot is taken. I'm going around in circles, trying to find a place to dump the van.

Then I notice Booth's truck with the American flag hogging up two spaces. Nice.

I ease my foot off the brake, sort of bumping my way into that narrow parking space. I'm almost there. Okay. I've got this. Just as I'm celebrating my first day behind the wheel, I hear the cringeworthy groan of my fender scraping against the truck's bumper.

Shit.

I get out and survey the damage. The truck's nasty green paint is blotched all across Dad's fender. This is bad. Really bad. I try to rub it off with my fist, but it doesn't help. In fact, I'm probably making it worse, so I give up and start walking to the motel.

The old men are playing dominoes at their table. They watch in silence as I drift upstairs. Somebody whistles, but I don't turn around. Go ahead. Take a good luck at the freak. I scan the breezeway for Fruit Loop. She's gone and so is Mouse. That's what makes me nervous.

Before I reach the motel room, I get a whiff of fried meat and grease. Dad's cooking dinner. It smells so freaking delicious, I almost forget that I'm mad at him, but it's going to take more than rice and beans to get over his bullshit.

"Hey, needle legs," he says as I unlock the door.

Dad's back in his laugh track mode, grinning as he dumps a can of Goya beans into the Crock-Pot. He's got the electric skillet going. I almost fall over when I see the rubbery strips of beef. Are you kidding me? Where did he get the money for that?

"All good?" He sticks out his hand.

I stare at it.

He slowly lets it drop. "Listen," he says, cracking open a beer. He takes a long gulp and wipes the foam off his lips. "I know you're upset about what happened last night. Soon as I get a little cash, I'll buy you a new phone."

Dad's promises are worth less than my Super Glue boots.

"So you went on a little joyride?" he says.

God, he's going to kill me.

"I just went to school."

I wait for him to start yelling. Instead, he says, "I was scared to death. Do you know how dangerous that was?"

"Yeah, I know."

"Don't do it again." He gets this nervous look on his face. Suddenly, I understand why he's playing it cool.

He's afraid of losing control.

Dad's grip on me is slipping away. And he knows it. So now he's acting all nice, like we're friends again, but I'm not falling for his crap.

It won't last.

I put the car keys on the table. Sooner or later, he's going to notice the lime-green paint smeared on the bumper. I leave that part out for now.

"How was school?" he asks.

"Okay," I mumble.

"Did your friend show up?"

He means Mr. Plain White Tee.

"No, I didn't see him."

"Perfect," he says. "Let's hope he didn't see you. So what's the deal? Nothing happened?"

"Nothing."

There's no way I'm telling him about Mom. I'm not even going to open my mouth about Fruit Loop. Not until I figure this out.

The dumpster boombox is propped on the floor near the bed. I must be hallucinating because all the buttons are lit up. I twist the volume knob and a blast of salsa leaks out. The stupid thing actually works.

"Just like old times. Remember?" Dad winks.

Yeah, I remember this song. It's Celia Cruz, singing about la vida es un carnaval. Bad times will pass, if you just keep dancing. Does anybody really believe that?

"Come on," Dad says, shaking his hips.

"I don't feel like it."

He makes a face. "You too lazy?"

No. I'm too big to stand on your feet.

"Here," he says, handing me a paper plate. "Eat up."

I push the green peppers to the side. Dad knows they make me sick, but he dumps them on my rice anyway.

"So where did you get the money for this?"

He rubs his belly. "A man needs red meat."

This is so messed up. We're basically homeless and Dad's spending all our dumpster money on beer and red meat?

"What about the rent?" I ask.

Dad picks his teeth. "What about it?"

"You didn't pay Booth last week."

"I'll pay him. Soon enough."

I shove another forkful of shredded beef in my mouth. I need more time. If we get kicked out of the motel, it's game over. We'll be on the road again, sleeping in the van. I'll lose my chance to be free.

I'll lose everything.

There's no way I'm going to let that happen.

I crumple my plate into the garbage.

"No more?" Dad says like he can't believe it.

"I'm done."

The boombox thuds behind us. It's weird to think that Celia Cruz is long gone, but her voice never left the Earth. Up and down the lights on the stereo wiggle, keeping time with the beat. I get up and turn it off. Still, the music hangs over the motel room, lurking over me like a ghost.

14

Customers only," said the lady at the Texaco station.
"But it's an emergency. My little girl needs to go real
bad," Dad said, squeezing my hand.

I'd just turned ten. "Double digits," Dad said, but he still
treated me like a baby. I figured that's because we got more
stuff that way. Sometimes I felt like he wanted me to stay little
forever.

"Please," he said.

"You have to buy something first. Store policy," she said,
scratching her neck. The tips of her fingernails were filed into
raptor-like points.

Dad reached into his pocket and dumped a pile of quarters
on the counter. "What can I get with this?"

"Not much."

"Just give me a cup of coffee then."

The lady slumped over to the pot by the cash register. She
took her time filling the Styrofoam cup and slid it across the
counter.

I bet she helped herself to free coffee all day.

She handed Dad a key attached to a long chain. The plastic
card on the chain said, WOMEN, just in case we weren't sure.

"Thanks," Dad muttered.

As soon as we stepped outside, he splashed his coffee on
the grass.

"Why did you do that?" I asked.

He crushed the Styrofoam cup in his fist. "I already know
it's no good."

The restroom at the gas station was small. Real small. That's
because Dad was standing behind me while I peed. When I
finished, I grabbed a bunch of paper towels and dipped them

under the faucet. It had been a long time since I'd had a real bath.

Dad pushed his way up to the sink. "Can you do my back?" he said, yanking off his T-shirt.

When I was little, I used to love washing my dad's back. The curve of his spine like beads on a chain. His shoulder blades, sharp as bird wings. Now the sight of his half-naked body made me embarrassed.

"Come on," he said, handing me a paper towel.

I scrubbed Dad's back, tracing circles around his scars, all the tea-colored welts.

A jellyfish.

That's how it happened.

I couldn't picture Dad swimming in the ocean. Couldn't imagine the sting of the jellyfish, their tentacles hooking into his skin. Still, he never turned his gaze away from the shore. It was the first time he saw a beach in real life. He didn't know it would be so dangerous.

Mom was there with him. When she floated in the ocean, I was floating inside her too. The boats drifted off the horizon. Their lights were stars tumbling into the sea. The waves swarmed with jellyfish.

"All of a sudden, they were everywhere," he told me.

"Were you scared?"

"Yeah. But I'm stronger than them."

"Am I strong too?"

"The strongest of all."

A jellyfish doesn't look so strong.

Dad said we'd have a new house with a pool. I could go swimming all day. No scary jellyfish to worry about.

"A pool is a lot better than the beach anyway."

Unless you're a jellyfish.

15

For the rest of the week at school, I hide in the bathroom. If Mr. Plain White Tee wants to play hide-and-seek, I can play too. Or maybe I'm just paranoid. He's looking for another kid. A stoner who bought a dime bag from the wrong person. Or maybe that cop's just waiting for the perfect moment to catch me.

On Friday I fail two quizzes. My research paper is non-existent. The only class I'm surviving in is calculus. *The study of change*, Mr. Toth always writes on the board. All I do is show up and grind out the answers. If only my life was that easy.

At lunchtime, I go to the library like I always do. The ceiling drips as if I'm in a cave deep underground. I drag out a chair and plunk myself in front of a computer. Still no word from Mom. She's got to check her Facebook once in a while. Maybe she hasn't read my message yet. At least, that's what I hope. Otherwise there's only one reason why she hasn't written back.

She's ignoring me.

I've got a couple of random messages from people I don't know. For some reason, all these middle-aged dudes want to be my "friend."

How are you today? Maybe we could chat....

I don't have a profile picture, but that won't stop them. God, they must be desperate. I scroll through my inbox, clicking away.

subject: FRIEND OF YOUR MOTHER

My breath catches in my throat. For a minute, I sit there, blinking at the message on the screen. Then I click on it.

I want to talk to you...

That's what guys always say.

Listen. We get hundreds of emails from strangers. I'm talking letters. Phone calls. You name it. Every time that stupid TV show has an update on missing kids. How do we know you're her daughter?

We?

If you're for real, let's meet up tonight.
—Kareem

I squint at his profile pic, but I can't get a glimpse of his face. Just a wedge of teeth and an afro that swells around the frame. Mom's friend.

Does he mean "friend" like boyfriend? Or something else? The message was sent a couple hours ago. I click on his Facebook page, but no dice. It's private. Can I trust this guy? What's his deal anyway? Maybe he's just another creeper looking for a "friend"? If he's legit, why didn't Mom write back to me herself? Maybe he's trying to protect her.

I stare at the words on the screen until my eyes burn.

Dear Kareem: Yes, I can meet you. Here's the deal. I'll go ONLY if I get to pick the place. Deal?

I hit SEND.

Lunch is almost over. I need to get to class soon. I lean back in my hard plastic chair and try to remember how to breathe. Then a checkmark pops up next to my message.

SEEN AT 12:34PM.

Wait. Did he read my message already?

Minutes pass. I gawk at the screen as if I could zap myself through the invisible electrons to the other side.

Deal.
Tell me where.

The words glow inside the message box. Kareem's on the other side right now, waiting for my answer. Maybe he's glued to a computer in an office. Whatever. I've got his attention. I won't let him get away.

Where can I meet this guy? I'm not bringing him to the

motel, that's for sure. It's got to be somewhere close. In other words, a public place within walking distance. I don't have a lot of options, but there's one spot that might work.

Domino Park.

I wouldn't exactly call it a park. More like a cabana where the old dudes chomp on cigars and clack dominos across the tables. It's not too far from the Surfside. I could walk there from the motel. Only one problem. How am I supposed to sneak away from Dad?

A couple seconds later, the screen lights up.

I get off work late tonight. Meet @ 10pm. You show up alone. Understand? Just you. Nobody else. Or it's over.

I type OK and hit SEND before I change my mind and back out.

What the hell am I doing? This is crazy. And why do I have to show up alone? Kareem might be a face-eating zombie. Or a serial killer who's going to chop me up and toss my fingers and toes into Biscayne Bay.

Ever since I was little, Dad's taught me not to trust anyone.

This time, I don't have a choice.

Class is finally over. As I step into the hallway, my stomach burns. I'm so hungry, I'm going to puke. How is this even possible? There's nothing inside me. I lean over the water fountain and suck down the lukewarm stream.

"You really shouldn't drink that water, snake bite."

I lift my head.

Shawn's leaning against the wall behind me. "No clue what's in it."

"Thanks for the tip," I say, walking over to him. "Next time you sneak up on me like that, give me a warning."

"Deal," he says. "So how come you disappeared all week?"

A jolt tingles through me. It feels so weird talking to Shawn at school, especially after all we shared. School is another dimension. A cold, dead planet on the edge of the universe. No sign of intelligent life.

"I sort of skipped half my classes. Not on purpose," I tell him, just in case he thinks I'm a loser.

"So it was accidental skipping?"

"Something like that."

"Hey, I seriously thought you were avoiding me," he says as we push through the double doors into the blazing sunlight. "You never got my texts?"

Now I feel bad. "Sorry. My dad took my phone away. I wasn't avoiding you, I swear."

"That sucks."

"Well, that pretty much sums it up." I leave out the part about Dad smashing my phone into a million pieces.

"You still down for a boat ride?" he asks.

"Right now?"

"The time is now. My sister let me borrow the Tank. Her classes got cancelled today so she's at Dolphin Mall with her capitalist friends. We should take advantage. Unless you're not into it—"

"I'm into it," I tell him.

Actually, this isn't true. I've never been on a boat in my entire life. And water isn't exactly my friend. I'm standing there like an idiot, trying to figure out what to do. That's when I spot Mr. Plain White Tee. He's watching from behind the D.A.R.E. fence. His eyes meet mine and I quickly look away.

Shawn nudges me. "So are we doing this or what?"

"Yeah, let's go."

As we head toward the parking lot, I look over my shoulder. Mr. Plain White Tee has disappeared again. Now I'm really scared. Just because I don't see him, it doesn't mean he's gone. He could be watching from a parked car. Or the bleachers on the field.

He could be everywhere.

❧

The bay sparkles in the late afternoon sun. As we walk to the docks, an egret swoops into a tree. The gnarled roots stretch like hands above the waves.

"Is that a mangrove tree?" I ask Shawn.

He nods. "The one and only."

I remember what he told me. Mangrove seeds float all over the world. The traveling trees.

I'm holding my breath when we reach the end of the dock. I can't even look down at the water. My heart is thudding like crazy. How am I going to get through this? Meanwhile, Shawn is kneeling on the edge, unwinding a thick coil of rope, like it's no big deal.

"Your dad doesn't care if we steal his boat?" I ask.

Shawn grins. "I wouldn't call it stealing."

"Okay. You mean borrowing without permission?"

He tosses the rope. "I don't need permission if it's mine."

Wait.

This boat belongs to Shawn?

It reminds me of a pocketknife, all sleek edges and gleaming metal trim. My dad's old boss, Hutch, had a crappy little fishing boat back in Orlando. I never saw him take it anywhere. Mostly, it just rotted in the backyard. He acted like that piece of shit was a fancy yacht, but this is the real deal.

"I never met anyone with their own private yacht," I say, trying to make a joke. Somehow it comes out wrong.

"A yacht's twice as big," he says, stepping onto the boat. "This is just a bowrider. Only eighteen feet."

"Well, how am I supposed to know?" I snap.

He looks away.

Now I'm acting stupid again. I'm sort of intimidated by all this stuff. The big glass house. The bowrider or whatever it's called.

Shawn stretches out his hand. "All aboard."

I stare at that shimmering water, unable to move.

"What?" he says. "Are you scared?"

Yeah, I'm scared.

Because I can't swim.

It's a rich people thing, swimming. I didn't grow up with a pool in my backyard, and besides, I couldn't afford lessons. So, yeah. I never learned how to swim. If I fall in that water, I'm fish food.

A long time ago, Dad tried to teach me how to swim. There was a canal behind the yellow house. Nothing fancy. More like a big puddle. He threw me in and laughed as I doggy-paddled, gasping for breath.

"You either sink or swim in this world."

That's what he told me.

"Come on, 'fraidy cat," says Shawn.

I still don't take his hand. "I'm not afraid."

"Then prove it."

I reach out and grab hold. God, I can't believe I'm going through with this. I've got one foot on the dock, the other on the boat. I glance down at the sunlight crackling across the tide. "Don't let go, okay?"

"I won't," he says. "And you don't have to squeeze so hard. I'm starting to lose circulation."

As I step down, I sort of tumble against him. For a moment, we stand there, holding on. This would be the perfect time to kiss him. Or crack a joke, at least. But I don't know what I'm supposed to do.

Shawn gently lets go. "Want to drive? I'll show you once we get out on the water."

"I thought we were already on the water."

"You're funny. You know that?"

"Sometimes I need to be reminded."

"Okay. Remind me to remind you." He grabs a life jacket off the bench and tosses it at me. "Here's your basic personal flotation device. Put it on so you don't drown."

The life jacket has so many buckles, I almost strangle myself trying to wiggle into it. "This doesn't seem very basic."

"Not after you've turned it into spaghetti." He guides my arm through the strap. This is getting really awkward.

"So how far away is this secret location?"

"No worries. It's super close," he says, taking out his keys. I didn't even know boats had keys.

The engine rumbles as we slowly back away from the docks. The sun feels good warming up my skin. So does the breeze, tinged with the smell of low tide. I close my eyes and gulp it in.

"I started boating lessons when I was fourteen," Shawn explains as we pick up speed. "My parents gave me this Sea-Ray last year for my birthday."

"Does it have a name?"

"Not yet," he says. "I probably should've named her a long time ago."

Another boat rumbles across the bay. There's a woman in big red sunglasses on the upper deck, waving like we're old friends. I try to imagine what she sees. That rich lady doesn't know I live in a motel. All she sees is a girl in the sunshine, waiting for what comes next.

"Want to take over?" Shawn asks.

I sink back to reality. "You mean drive?"

"Yes, drive."

"But I don't know how."

He puts his hands on my shoulders and guides me over to the steering wheel. "Wind's pretty good right now. Not too much spray. We're going to plane out in a minute. Can you handle that?"

I have no clue what he's talking about. The dashboard's got all these knobs and dials. I'm scared of pushing the wrong button.

"What happens if we crash?"

"You won't crash into anything out here," he says, waving at the open sea. He pushes the throttle forward. Now we're picking up speed. The front of the boat is lifting, as if it might take off into the air. Not going to lie—this is scary as hell, but it's also really exciting. Shawn points at the horizon. "I think we're being followed."

A dark wedge of fin splashes above the surface of the water.

Another pops up a couple feet away. Then another. We're surrounded by dolphins.

"They're curious about us," he says, leaning over the edge of the boat. "Hey, Mr. Dolphin. What's up?"

I've never seen anything like this. Not in my entire life. All those fins and tails skimming the water. For a while, we stay quiet. There's just the sunlight crackling off Biscayne Bay. Shawn's hands on my shoulders. The secret fins that belong to dolphins and all that's hidden below the curl of the waves.

Please God. Don't take this away.

The boat tips down. Now we're gliding across the bay. I grip the steering wheel so tight, my knuckles burn. I've never felt in control before. Never felt like anything belonged to me. Maybe not the entire world. Just enough to hold close.

We're not far from the shore, yet the city feels miles away. I can't stop looking at the water, how it shifts between green and blue. Then I notice something rising up in the distance. Something so big, there's no way it's another boat.

It's a house.

"Welcome to Stiltsville," says Shawn. "Back in the day, these houses used to be a secret hide-out for pirates. This is the Springs House, one of the last survivors. The rest got wiped out in Hurricane Andrew."

"Do people actually live here?"

"Not unless they get caught."

As we drift closer, more houses seem to float above the water. Most are just candy-colored shacks dotted with seagulls. The Springs House is definitely the most breathtaking. It's got a deck on the second floor and a bunch of rope swings, as well as a brightly painted mural of King Triton.

"Okay, snake bite. I'm going to take it from here." Shawn grabs hold of the steering wheel. Slowly, we begin to turn toward the dock.

Up close, the stilt-house is even bigger than I imagined. I watch the gulls lift off, one by one, and settle on the roof. What does it feel like to stretch your wings and fly? They soar without a sound, dangling on invisible strings.

"Hi there, birds," I say, wiggling my fingers. "I always wave like they're going to wave back."

"Watch out for the sea turkeys. They'll tear you limb from limb."

"My dad calls them sky rats."

Shawn laughs. "Maybe that's what I should name the bow-rider."

"That's a weird name for a boat."

"Yeah, but weird names are sort of a requirement," he says, leaning in.

He kisses me as the seagulls wheel above us. At that moment, I let go of everything. All the hurt I've been holding inside, clenched tight like a fist.

Then I fly.

16

You're a tough old house, aren't you?" I whisper.
I try to imagine Stiltsville back in the day. Out here,
you're free. No rules. Nobody bossing you around. It's
the perfect hiding spot for bad guys.

"Feels like we're walking the plank," Shawn says, as the dock
sways beneath our feet.

I glance down at the water. "Ever see any jellyfish?"

"That was random. And, yeah, there's tons of jellyfish."

"Great." I shiver.

We walk to the deck, where a couple of plastic chairs face the
bay, as if waiting for us. I can't help touching the shells nailed to
the wall. Starfish. A bleached-white sand dollar. A seahorse so
tiny and perfect, it might wiggle free and swim away.

"Are we going inside?" I ask.

"Actually, we're going up."

I follow Shawn up the long wooden steps to the second
floor. When we reach the deck, I lean against the railing and
gaze out at Key Biscayne. The water is smooth as a tarp. Where
are those dolphins now? Maybe they were magic, after all.

Shawn swings his leg over the railing, as if he's about to
jump. Then he stands up and pulls himself onto the roof.

"You really are insane," I tell him.

"What can I say? I like heights."

"If you die, it's not my fault."

"I won't die. At least, not today," he says, unlacing his sneakers. "Are you coming or what?"

"Me? I'm not going up there."

"Why not?"

"Because it's crazy."

"You scared?"

"I'm never scared."

Okay. That's not exactly true. In fact, it's sort of the opposite of true. Still, it's hard to resist a challenge.

I climb onto the deck railing and Shawn helps me onto the roof. "God, I can't believe I'm doing this."

Together we stand on the edge of nowhere, looking at the bay.

"Ready?" he says.

"For what?"

"We're going to jump."

"We?"

He's already tugging off his shirt. "Yes, we."

I don't want him to see the bites on my legs. The swollen bruises. The welts I scratched until my fingernails were rimmed with blood.

"It's no big deal," Shawn says. He can probably tell I'm nervous. "You don't have to jump if you don't want to."

"I want to."

At that moment, I'm not lying. I want to swim with Shawn in that clear blue water, but I'm so embarrassed. Slowly, I wiggle out of my jeans. Then I lift my T-shirt over my head. For a second, I hesitate. No going back. I pull off the bandana that hides my Stain. I'm right there. All of me.

He's watching the whole time, but I don't mind. In fact, I like it. And I like looking at him too. His lean chest. The slope of his waist above his boxers. I've never taken off my clothes in front of a boy. Of course, I'm still wearing my bra and panties. That's sort of like a bathing suit. Yet somehow it's not the same.

"You forgot your socks," he says.

I look down at my feet.

Now we're both laughing again.

Shawn grabs my hand. "On the count of three, okay?"

"No. Wait." I'm starting to panic. What if there's jellyfish in the water?

"It's now or never."

"Promise you won't let go. I mean, that's the classic trick, right? I jump. And you stand there, laughing at me."

One.

"I won't do that, I swear."

Two.

"You better not."

"Reece, I promise I won't let go."

"I mean it. For real."

"Do you trust me?" he says.

I stare down at that water.

Three.

I push off. My legs circle the air, but there's nothing. Only the sky and Shawn's fingers laced with mine. We hit the water so hard, it stings. I let go as we plummet into a world of murky green. Then my toes sink into the mud and seagrass and I kick my way toward sunlight.

I'm clean.

No motel shower ever felt this good. The water is soft as cream against my skin. God, can I just stay here forever? When I splash to the surface, I find Shawn stretched out in a chair on the deck.

"Thought I'd have to call a search party," he says as I climb up.

....you either sink or swim in this world...

"Reece?"

"Sorry," I tell him. "Was I spacing out again?"

He kisses my forehead. "You're a pretty amazing girl. You know that?"

"No, actually I didn't."

"Well, I did," he says, laughing. "So tell me. What don't I know?"

"About what?"

"You," he says.

My head throbs. I feel like I'm going to pass out. I could give him some bullshit story. Me and Dad used to practice all the time. I didn't get to choose. He told me what to say. I was adopted when I was a baby. He was my "uncle," watching over me.

It's time I stopped lying.

"My family used to travel around a lot," I tell him.

"For real? You mean like on vacation?"

"My parents were...nomads."

"Nomads?"

I've never told anybody before.

"That's crazy. Your family lived off the grid or something?"

"They were always traveling around, looking for work. And...I don't know. Maybe hoping for a better life."

For a moment, we're both quiet.

"Where did you grow up?" he asks.

"Nowhere." I scoot my legs over the edge of the dock, where they dangle above the water, swinging in circles.

"Okay. I get it." He's starting to lose patience with me. "You moved around a lot. But where are you from?"

"I'm me, I guess."

Whatever that means.

"You say that like it's weird."

"It's not weird," I say, a little offended. The words come out fast and mean. I don't even recognize my own voice. Why do I sound so angry?

I am angry.

As the boat steers toward Key Biscayne, the sun's low, almost melting into the bay. I don't want this to end. Don't want to go back to that dirty motel room. I just want to stay here with Shawn forever. My T-shirt is damp against my shoulder blades. There's a softness leftover from the sea.

"The sun's about to go down," Shawn tells me, shielding his face with his hand.

"Sunsets are an optical illusion. You know. Like the green flash."

"The green what?"

"If you watch the sun set on the ocean, you're supposed to see a green flash at the last second."

"Did you ever see it?"

"No."

"Then how do you know it's real?"

We squint at the horizon.

Shawn puts his arm around me. "Where's your magical green flash?"

"Be patient." I lean into him, my gaze on the fading sky. The sun goes down, slowly melting into the water, until it finally disappears. Same as every day. Nothing magical about it.

"So this flash," he says, holding me close. "Is it like a special thing? Or does it happen all the time?"

"You have to be in the right place." Yeah, like I know what I'm saying. All I can think about is Shawn, his fingers on my hips. The rise and fall of the boat, keeping time with the waves.

"Who says you're not in the right place?" He kisses my neck.

All too soon, the glass house rises in the distance, the windows glowing against the sky. I've lived in so many places, but I've never seen skies this big before. So big, they could swallow us up. And that's okay with me.

When we reach the dock, Shawn steps off and ties up the boat. He does it so easily, like it's second nature. Guess it's no big deal, if you've grown up around water your whole life.

"After you, my lady," he says, offering his hand.

"You think I'm going to fall in?"

He smirks. "If you fall, I'm not jumping in to rescue you."

"Too bad. Because that would be really funny."

"Not as funny as you falling in." He reaches for my hand. This time, I grab hold. I'm so used to taking care of myself. For once I'm letting my guard down. It doesn't mean I'm not strong. Not if it's my choice.

Together we walk toward the house. A gust of wind picks up, clattering the palm fronds, and all of a sudden, I'm cold. I don't want to go back to the motel, but Dad's probably freaking out and I'm in enough trouble right now. I'm supposed to meet Kareem at Domino Park in a few hours.

"What time is it?" I ask.

Shawn grins. "Time for you to chill. What's the rush?"

"Can you give me a ride home?" I ask.

He looks disappointed. "Sure you don't want to stay for dinner? You're missing out on the world's greatest elote. I mean, come on. Is there anything better than grilled corn with cheese?"

My stomach clenches. Maybe I'm starting to hallucinate, but I swear the breeze smells like barbeque smoke.

"Okay," I tell him. "But I can't stay long."

"You won't regret it. I promise."

He leads me through the bead-draped palms into the backyard. The scent of charred wood sharpens the air. I'm not hallucinating after all. On the wood-paneled deck extending from the house, there's a grill bright with flames, and behind it, a tall dark-haired man.

Shawn's dad.

I didn't picture him like this. Flip-flops and jeans. A close-cropped beard shadowing his grin.

"Reece, yes?" he says. "My son's told me a lot about you."

Not too much, I hope.

I step onto the deck, blinking through the heat. The charred smoke is making me a little dizzy. Or maybe I'm just super nervous. I don't want to do something stupid, so I smile and hope that's enough.

Shawn plops down into a chair. "My dad's the grill master. There's nothing he can't roast over an open fire. Jalapeño poppers. Big freaking ears of corn. Watermelon. You name it."

Mr. Bryant laughs. "The donuts didn't quite work out."

"At least we tried. That's half the battle."

Shawn seems really tight with his dad. Almost like they're friends. A pang of envy shoots through me. If only my dad was this cool. We never had a barbeque or anything like that. Not unless you count the time Dad scorched a tinfoil-wrapped lump of ground beef on the van's engine.

Mrs. Bryant glides out through a sliding glass door, looking elegant as always in her flowy black pants and long-sleeved blouse. "So glad to see you again," she says, setting a tray down on the table. And I believe it. Believe that she's actually glad I'm here, gulping the smoke on her deck.

Not half as glad as me.

Shawn leans in and whispers, "You're really lucky, snake bite. You know that? Because my dad found out you were coming over today. And he doesn't cook for just anybody."

"You told him?"

"Yeah, maybe I did." His eyes meet mine, then shift to the beaded palms swaying above the deck.

I'm so surprised, I don't know what to say. Let's be real. It's always been me and Dad. How could I ever get close to somebody else? And now here I am. My first real barbeque. Achievement unlocked. Shawn passes me a grilled corn and he's right. It's amazing. Why didn't I have this in my life before? I crunch through one, then reach for another.

"Man, you're a corn-eating machine," he says, laughing.

I'm so busy stuffing my face, it takes a second before I see Emily. She's marching toward us, stomping across the grass.

"You," she says, jabbing her finger at me. "Did you think I wouldn't find out? I mean, did you really think I was that stupid?"

Shawn looks at me, then his sister. "What's going on?"

"Your new girlfriend's a thief," she says.

I feel like I'm going to throw up. All the blood inside me is swooshing around. I can barely hear what she's saying. New girlfriend. Is that what she said? How many girlfriends does Shawn have?

He holds up his hands. "Can you stop talking for one second? Let me get this straight. You think Reece stole your bracelet?"

"I know she did."

"You've got, like, a million bracelets and you're always leaving them all over the house. How do you know she took it?"

"Because she was in the kitchen by herself. Then it was gone."

Shawn looks at me. "This is all a big mistake, right?"

His mom and dad are watching. I really wanted them to like me. Now I've destroyed everything. If I had some kind of superpower, I would zap myself back in time. Rewind the past. Leave that gold bracelet on the table. Turn and walk away. But there's nothing I can do.

Nothing except tell the truth.

"Yes, I took her bracelet," I say, lowering my head. "It was stupid. I don't even know why I did it."

Emily rolls her eyes. "You don't know?"

"I'm really sorry."

"Yeah," she says. "Sorry you got caught."

No doubt, Shawn's family hates me right now. I can't go back and change what I did. Maybe it's too late to fix it, but I've got to try.

"Let me show you where it is."

I walk over to the tall grass near the boat dock. The bracelet's got to be here somewhere. I get on my hands and knees, scraping my fingers through the dirt.

Please let it be here.

"Is this some kind of joke?" Emily says.

I'm about to give up, then I notice something metallic in the grass, catching the light. I reach down and grab it.

Emily snatches the bracelet away from me and shoves it over her wrist. "So you chickened out at the last minute? Is that why you threw it away?"

I stand and wipe the mud off my jeans. When I took that bracelet, it wasn't a conscious thing. Ever since I was little, Dad has trained me to take whatever I could find. I stare at the bracelets clacking down her arms—so many, I couldn't count them all.

Do your thing.

Emily waits for my answer. Why would she understand? She's never scraped rotten hamburger meat out of the garbage. Chewed it real slow so it lasts. Prayed to the dumpster gods she doesn't get sick.

"I'm sorry."

That's all I can say.

Shawn's dad walks over. I wait for him to start yelling. That's exactly what my dad would do. But his voice is gentle when he says, "I think you need to leave."

At that moment, I want to die. I wish the ground would split open and swallow me up. If the earth is hollow, now's my chance to find out.

I turn to Emily. "I'm really sorry about your bracelet."

She shrugs. "Whatever. It was fake gold anyway."

I watch her go back inside the house.

Shawn looks at me for a long time, then takes out his keys. He moves toward the car, keeping his gaze straight ahead. I almost wish he'd yell at me. Call me a thief.

His silence hurts more than anything he could say.

17

On the drive home, Shawn leaves the windows open. The street noise pounds against my skin, sharp, yet too quiet, all at once. The traffic lights never looked so distant. All those cars in a hurry to go somewhere else.

"You probably hate me right now."

Shawn's driving at light speed, like he can't wait to get rid of me. "God, I really thought you were different."

The words cut through me.

"I'm sorry I let you down." No matter how many times I say, "I'm sorry," it's never enough.

He turns his head. "What's the deal with you, Reece? Do you always go around stealing stuff? Is that, like, your game or something?"

"It's not a game."

This is how I survive.

"I mean, seriously. You were stealing junk from the gas station when I met you. I thought you were this little badass. I was like, damn. I need to get to know this girl. Now I wish we never met."

I flinch. "Don't say that."

"I brought you over to my house. Do you know what a big deal that is? My parents are super old-school. Shit. My sister wasn't allowed to date until she turned eighteen."

"Please. Just give me a chance to explain."

"Explain what?" He's shouting at me. I've never seen him so pissed off. If I could crawl under the seat and hide, I would do it.

"I'm sorry my life isn't perfect like yours."

He wipes his eyes. "You think my life is perfect?"

"It sort of looks that way."

"Well, you're wrong."

"I'm not trying to hurt you. It's just…" I try to put it into words. "I'm really jealous, okay? I never had anything like that."

"What? You mean a big house on the water? Is that what you're saying? Oh, those rich people from Key Biscayne?"

"No. I'm jealous because your family actually cares about you."

He opens his mouth, as if he's about to say something. Then he sort of slumps behind the wheel.

"Think about it, Shawn. Do you know how lucky you are? Your mom was so nice to me. And your sister is awesome. I'm sure she hates me too. And that really sucks because I was kind of hoping we'd be friends."

"Then why did you screw it up?"

I can't answer him. There are no answers. At least, none that make sense.

He heaves a sigh. "For the record, my family's not perfect. Most of the time, I never see my dad. I come home from school and zone out on the Xbox. Crank the volume real loud so I don't have to listen to the noise inside my head."

"I know how that feels."

"For real?"

"You basically just described my whole life."

Shawn stares out the windshield at the motel. "So you're not going to explain this to me?" he says, waving at the motel's neon lights. "Don't you think I deserve to know what's going on?"

"Yeah, you do." I really want to tell him the truth. It's right there, hovering on the surface. I'm so sick of carrying this secret.

Still, I keep quiet.

"Fine." Shawn cuts the ignition. He gets out of the car and walks over to the passenger door. When he yanks it open, my throat tightens up. Why does he have to be so nice all the time?

"Please don't hate me."

"I don't hate you," he says and for some reason, I believe him. "I just don't think we should be together right now."

I'm crying for real. No holding back. "Just give me a chance."
Shawn looks away. "Goodbye, Reece."
I feel like I've been kicked. All the breath knocked out. As I
walk across that motel parking lot, I'm thinking about Shawn,
how he opened up to me. The hurt in his voice, the way it
cracked when he said goodbye.

This was my one chance at normal. For the first time, I was
part of a world that didn't revolve around my dad. It belonged
to me, if only for a limited time. And then I destroyed everything.

I didn't deserve it.

"Hi there, blondie."

I glance up. Somebody's blocking the stairs. That burnt rubber smell. It's the creepy guy next door. God, please make him
go away.

"You're not going to say hi?" He lurches in front of me.
His face is all sweaty, as if he just ran an Olympic marathon,
and he's grinding his teeth like he's on coke. And I don't mean
the kind you drink. "What's your problem?" he says, stroking
my hair. I can't believe he's actually touching me. I try to scoot
around him, but he's up in my space.

He grabs my hair and tugs. Hard. "Think you're better than
everybody else?"

I try to wrench myself free of his grip. "Let go."

"Says who? The motel princess?"

Motel princess?

That's some quality bullshit.

I take a step backward and crash against the wall. There's nowhere to go. I'm trapped beside the long row of motel rooms.
All those numbers. And not one door is going to open.

"Don't scream," he says, glancing over his shoulder at the
parking lot.

I've never been very good at following orders. So when he
says, "Don't scream," that's exactly what I do.

"Shut up." He yanks my head back. I'm looking at the second floor, where Mouse is on the ledge, clutching her plastic

doll. "You're going to move slowly," he says, pushing me away from the stairs. "Got that, blondie?"

There's nothing behind the motel except for a vacant lot, the dirt sparkling with broken glass. No way in hell am I going in there.

"Move." He shoves me forward.

"Let go of me."

When I stumble, he pushes me against the wall. "I've seen you and your dad," he says. "Seen you crawling in the dumpster like a couple of rats. You go around here, acting like you're better than everybody else. Yeah, like you're some kind of god-damned princess. But you're just a piece of garbage."

His words hook under my skin. The hurt scrapes deep. Cuts me where it counts. I twist away from him. "I'm not garbage."

The guy clamps down on my neck and squeezes. I can't suck in a breath. I'm sinking underwater, the dark waves crashing over me. Everything melts away—the pain zinging through my skull, the distant hum of the fluorescent lights.

"Get your hands off her," somebody yells.

I can't see his face, but I know it's Shawn.

He didn't leave after all.

Shawn's tall, but he's not very big. I can't imagine him trying to get violent with somebody. That's why I'm totally blown away when he swings back and pounds his fist into the tweaker.

As I sink to the ground, the guy lunges at Shawn and pummels him. I don't even see it coming. I mean, he's like a super-fast zombie. I don't know if it's the crank jacking up his system or what. Shawn crumples onto the ground. His legs kick and scrape at the pavement. I want to scream, but nothing comes out.

I have to do something.

Fast.

I sprint over to the dumpster, reach inside, and pull out a beer bottle. It's empty, but it feels solid in my grip. I don't waste any time thinking about it. I swing as hard as I can at the guy's skull.

He lets out a groan and slumps forward. The bottle doesn't even break. It slips out of my fingers and clatters across the parking lot.

Shawn coughs and sort of flops onto his side. Slowly, he crawls to his knees. He's alive. Barely.

"Come on," I say, pulling him toward the stairs. Everything's in slow motion as I drag him up the steps to the second floor. Mouse has disappeared. She must've gone back to her place to hide. Can't say I blame her.

As we move past the rows of doors, my head's throbbing like a grenade that's about to explode. I don't want to go inside that room, but I have no choice.

The door swings open.

When I hit the light switch, I almost wish I'd left it off.

You can't even tell that human beings live here. The bed is totally stripped. No blankets. Not even a pillowcase. The mattress is slumped against the bathroom door like a dead body. My clothes are scattered all over the floor, the pockets of my jeans turned inside-out. Dad was looking for money. How do I know? Because he tore this place to shit.

"Welcome to the Surfside." I tip the mattress over and sit down.

"It's okay," Shawn says.

"It's not okay."

I don't know if it's his voice, so soft and reassuring. Or the way he's holding me close, just letting me be. I'm fighting back tears. Why can't I have a normal life? Right now, it feels like nothing will ever be normal again.

He sinks next to me. "What's going on, Reece? You can't hide forever. Why won't you let me help?"

I want Shawn's help.

"Don't you trust me?" he says.

"You're the only one I trust."

"Then why do you keep acting like I'm the bad guy? I'm not trying to hurt you, I swear. I just want to understand." He droops forward, like he's going to puke. Then he looks down at his hand. "I think I broke a finger."

"You're lucky that's all you broke."

He rubs his forehead. "Tell me about it."

"You're supposed to punch like this," I say, holding up my fist. "Why didn't your dad teach you?"

Shawn stares at the floor. "My dad's not exactly Stone Cold Steve."

Now I feel bad all over again.

"Hold on," I tell him.

I get up and make my way to the bathroom. For a second, I think Dad's hiding in there. He's gone, but the cabinet above the sink is flung wide open. Every squeezable thing dumped out. Toothpaste smeared across the mirror. All I want is a clean towel. I guess toilet paper will have to do.

I crumple up a wad of TP and dip it under the faucet. Then I walk back to the mattress on the floor. Shawn's zipped into his hoodie like a monk, his shoulders pressed against the wall.

"Let me check your wounds," I say, wiping the blood off his cheekbone. He's got a little gash on his forehead, but the cut isn't deep. My dad's been in plenty of fights. That's why I know it looks worse than it is.

"Am I going to live?" Shawn asks.

"I think you'll survive."

"What about you?" he says, looking up at me.

It hurts.

Dad said I wouldn't feel the match. He told me it's like a bee sting. One little bite and it's over.

He lied.

I'm screaming. All the breath inside me gone.

"Want the bad guys to find us?" he says, twisting my face. "You have to get rid of that thing."

My luna moth wings.

"Stop it." I kick his hand away. He's so strong, I can't do

anything. Can't even scream in the back of the van. There's nobody around to hear me.

The smell is everywhere. My skin bubbling black as marshmallow crust. But I won't see until later. Not until Dad makes me look in the rearview mirror, as if the pain has already faded into the distance.

It took this long to figure out the truth. Why didn't I see it before? I didn't know until now.

Dad's the bad guy.

☙

"I want to talk to you." The words spill out. I barely recognize my own voice. "But you can't tell anyone, okay?"

Shawn nods.

No turning back.

I take a deep breath. "When I was little, my parents fought a lot."

"Everybody's parents fight."

Not like mine.

"The fights were getting out of control. I was too little to understand. One night, Dad came into my room. He said we were taking a trip."

Shawn's listening hard. "How old were you?"

Good question.

I wasn't in first grade yet. But here's the thing. Dad pulled me out of school so many times, I lost track. Every time we moved, I kept switching grades. After a while, they all blended together.

"I'm not even sure what my age is now."

"What do you mean?" Shawn looks confused. "I don't understand. How come you don't know?"

"Because my dad took me away."

"You're saying that your dad…" Shawn trails off, shaking his head. "He kidnapped you?"

The word *kidnapped* makes me think of pirates. Argh. Walk the plank and all that crap. It doesn't come close to what Dad did to me.

He kidnapped my life.

"Dad took me away when I was little. He said my mom was dead. But he lied."

"Why?"

Shawn waits for my answer. I don't even know what to say. Can't put it into words. How am I supposed to explain that my entire reality is a lie? I'm aching to tell him the truth, but I can't find the words.

"We've been hiding for years."

"Hiding from what?"

"I'm not really sure." Am I hiding from my mom? Or something else? The "bad guys" who whispered in the pines the night we ran away?

Shawn puts his arm around me and I sort of collapse against him. For a minute, we lean into each other, saying nothing.

"You don't have to hide anymore," he tells me.

I wish that I believed him.

"So what am I supposed to do? I can't go to the police. They're going to put my dad in jail."

"Your dad belongs in jail."

Maybe it's true.

Still, I can't do this to Dad.

"Reece, listen to me. You have to get out of here," Shawn says, glancing around what's left of the motel room. "What about your mom? Do you know where she is?"

"I don't know."

"You have to find her."

"How?"

"Go online. Do a search or whatever."

"You think I haven't tried?"

"Try again," he says. "And keep trying. She's probably out there looking for you."

He's right.

Something rattles in the hallway. We both look up.

"You have to leave," he says. "Now."

I shake my head. "It's not that easy."

In my mind, I flash on the cop I saw at school. Mr. Plain White Tee. It's only a matter of time before he shows up at the motel.

"I just…can't."

Then the door swings open and Dad's standing there, his face glistening with sweat.

"Well, needle legs," he says, "the shit's finally hit the fan."

18

Dad marches into the room, but he leaves the door open. "You," he says, glaring at Shawn. "Get out." "Don't talk to him like that." I'm so pissed, I can't even breathe.

Shawn holds out his hand. "Come on, Reece," he says. "Let's go."

Now Dad's really losing it. His neck is splotched with rage, but his voice is strangely calm. "She's not going with you."

All my life, he's been the one in charge. Now it's my turn to make a decision. As much as I'm aching to walk out the door, I can't.

When I don't move, Shawn looks at me. "Are you going to be okay?"

I nod.

He glances back one more time.

Then he's gone.

Dad slides the lock on its chain. He was calm a minute ago. Too calm. Now it's full-on rage like I've never seen before.

"What the hell are you thinking?" he yells at me. "You weren't thinking. Not with your head, at least. You bring that boy over here and that's it. Game over. Want us to get caught?"

"Yeah, maybe I do."

He sort of teeters backward and collapses on the bed. Is he crying? In my entire life, I've only seen Dad cry once. Maybe twice.

The night we left.

And now.

He rubs his face. "We can't stay here."

That's obvious.

"We have to get on the road. But first I need to do something about your hair," he says, flicking it off my shoulders. "Maybe cut it a little shorter."

I jerk away from him. "Don't touch me."

"Fine," he says, holding up his hands. "What do you want then?"

"I want to see my mom."

You're just like her.

Dad pounds his fist against the wall. Go ahead. Throw another tantrum. He's shouting now. Pacing back and forth. Trying to make me believe his lies. "I put my ass on the line for you. I gave up everything."

"Actually, you took everything away."

"Yeah? Is that what you think? Well, it's time to move on. You hear me? That's the end of it."

"I'm not going."

He moves in front of the door. "What's your plan then? Think you can survive on your own? Without me, you're lost."

Lost?

What a freaking joke.

I've been lost for years.

"Tell me where Mom is."

"She doesn't want you, Reece. You were six years old when we left."

"You mean when you kidnapped me."

He stares. "Okay. I get it. I mean, yeah, I understand that you're upset. It's hard to—"

"Don't talk to me like that. I'm not a little kid."

"Well, you're not an adult."

"Then what am I?"

"You're…my daughter," he stammers.

There's something I need to ask. Something I've been wanting to ask since that night we drove away.

"Dad, what exactly are we hiding from?" I've been wanting to ask this question for so long. I never expected him to tell me the truth. He moves away from the door and sinks onto the mattress.

"I know it's hard to understand—"

"You said the 'bad guys' were after us."

"That's right."

"It's all bullshit, isn't it?"

He looks up. "What are you talking about?"

"You're the bad guy."

The room goes quiet as I watch my dad's lies fall apart.

"It was for your own good, Reece," he says.

"Do you really believe that?" I'm shaking so hard, I can barely spit out the words. "You think that kidnapping me was the right thing to do?"

"I was keeping you safe."

"Safe from what? I mean, for real. Who's going to keep me safe from you, Dad?"

Now he's pacing. The floor thuds with the rhythm of his movement. "You don't know anything."

"I know my mom is alive. Why didn't you tell me?"

He stays quiet.

"Were you in trouble when you left?"

Silence.

"You took her away from me, Dad. You took everything." I'm fighting back tears. "This is where we used to live, isn't it?"

"That's right," he says quietly. "You were born here in Miami."

The tree frogs sang at night.

After a thunderstorm, I heard their music.

This is my home.

"Why did we come back here?" I ask.

He sounds so pathetic when he finally says, "I thought maybe I could find work here. Yeah, it was a risk. But I thought maybe the others could help us out."

The others?

He means sky rats like us.

I'm not little anymore. He can't control my life. We've been running so long, he never thought about what happens next.

When I grew up.

"There was a show on TV."

"What show?" he snaps.

"About missing kids."

He mops the sweat off his face. "So?"

"My mom's still alive. And she's looking for me."

"Your mother doesn't give a shit about you, Reece. Who's been taking care of you, huh? All these years?"

"Everybody's looking for me."

Dad glances up. Now he's paying attention. "What did you say?"

"The lady down the hall...she knows."

"That old witch?"

"She knows who I am."

I push away my bandana and touch the Stain. My luna moth wings.

"We can't stay here," he says, pacing. "We've got twenty-four hours. Booth's kicking us out tomorrow."

"I'm not going with you."

Dad frowns. "If you run away, the cops will lock you up in juvie. Is that what you want?"

I've heard that before. It used to scare me, the thought of being locked up. But I'm already living in jail. The cop's been following me for days. It's only a matter of time before he shows up at the motel.

"Let me go, Dad."

He's really starting to freak. "Want to get yourself killed? Where the hell are you going to go?"

Good question.

I try to sound brave when I tell him, "I'll figure it out."

The silence hangs between us.

Dad turns to the door. He takes his time, unbolting the locks, one by one. Then he lifts his head and says, "Go. I won't stop you."

I stand perfectly still, looking at that motel door.

As if to prove his point, Dad yanks it open. The lights of the parking lot flare in the distance. Cold, empty light.

Ever since I can remember, I've been terrified of being alone. It was me and Dad all these years. I was terrified that something bad would happen to him. I'd come home from school and he'd be gone.

I'm not scared anymore.

I grab my Hail Kale bag. I don't have much, but it already feels too heavy. I walk up to Dad and he throws his arms around me. For a minute, we stay like that, just holding on. When I was little, we used to dance in the kitchen. I balanced on my dad's feet. Never on my own. I clung to him and tried not to fall.

Slowly, I let go.

Dad lowers his head as I walk out of the motel room. The breeze is damp and thick with heat, as if it might rain. He stands in the doorway, his face hidden by a shadow.

"Keep your eyes open, needle legs."

He locks the door.

19

All the stores are locked. I walk past the beauty supply place with the plastic heads stacked in the window. WE SELL 100% REAL HUMAN HAIR. Their painted mouths are smiling, but their bugged-out eyes are totally freaked.

I know exactly how they feel.

What if Kareem took off? Or worse. Maybe he doesn't really know my mom. This guy is just some random dude looking for a "friend." He's going to chop me up and feed me to the 'gators in the Everglades. At this point, I don't have a choice. He got my message online. This means he has to know something about Mom. Right now, he's the only one between me and the truth.

A bunch of old guys are slumped by the window at El Exquisito, gulping high-octane coffee out of Styrofoam cups. They're staring big time as I hustle toward Domino Park. Nobody else is around. The front gate is chained shut, the cabanas empty. All I see are palm trees in gravel studded with cigar butts.

I sink down on a bench. This is so messed up. I didn't make it in time. Kareem must've left already.

"You lost?" asks one of the old guys. His khaki pants are yanked to his armpits. I bet he irons the creases.

Yeah, that's me.

The lost girl.

"What time is it?"

He glances at his watch. Talk about a throwback. You never see anybody wear a real life watch anymore. "It's quarter past."

I always get confused when people say "quarter past." Finally, my brain catches up. It's pretty obvious Kareem's gone. I mean, if he showed at all. I glance at the old guys, their slicked-back hair and belted jeans. God, why can't I do anything right?

Even the old guys are laughing at my sorry ass. And none of these dudes look like the picture I saw online.

Well, I'm not going to sit here like an idiot. I'm out. I slide off the bench and start fast-walking to Thirteenth Avenue. In the middle of the block, a ceiba tree rises so high, its leaves drape the street lights. The dirt glints with pennies and dimes. Hundreds of prayers whispered under that tree. What did all those people wish for? Don't ask. Because it probably won't come true.

"Thought you weren't going to show up, Reece."

I spin around.

There's a man walking toward me. When I see him moving under the streetlight, I want to zap into another dimension. But I can't make myself disappear. Not this time.

"Kareem?"

Of course it's Kareem. He knows my name. At least, the name I've carried like a rope around my neck, ever since my braid floated in the stream.

"I waited," he says, like I owe him something.

"Well, I'm here now."

Kareem nods. "True, true."

He talks like he's from somewhere else—one of those vacation island type places. How would I know? I've never been there.

"It's just you? I mean, you came by yourself?" He glances at the road. In the distance, tires squeal down the street and we both flinch.

"It's just me." I hold up my hands.

"Good," he says, walking closer. He's got a backpack slung over his shoulder and sneakers so bright, his feet glow in the dark. This guy doesn't look like a face-eating zombie, but I can't let my guard down.

I stand near the ceiba, as if its branches will keep me safe. "Where's my mom? Why isn't she here too?"

"Because she doesn't know you exist."

"What?" My head's about to explode. This isn't exactly going the way I planned. "You didn't tell her about me?"

He shrugs. "You could be nobody."

"Why do you care?"

Kareem doesn't say anything. He gives me this weird look, as if he's trying to figure me out. "My wife gets emails from strangers every week. Ever since she went on that stupid TV show. It was starting to make her crazy. So I took over her Facebook page."

Did he say wife?

I tug off my bandana. Let him see my Luna moth wings. Still, Kareem doesn't move. "If you don't believe I'm for real," I say, looking at the coins in the dirt, "then why did you come here?"

"You're the first."

"The first?"

"None of the others bothered to show up."

Maybe he's lying. I want to trust him, but I'm not stupid. "So I'm supposed to believe you?"

He shrugs off his backpack and reaches inside. For a second, I think he's going to pull out a gun. All the blood inside me turns cold. Then he lifts up something that makes me shiver—a dress edged with lace.

"My First Communion dress."

"You remember." He sounds a little surprised. "Tell me, Reece. What else do you remember?"

I climbed the mango tree in that dress. It was part of me. Same as my music box and the guppies swirling in their tank. Now this man is holding it between us like a ghost. He's watching me. Waiting.

"So why now?" he asks.

"What do you mean?"

"You watched that TV show about missing kids."

"Yes," I say, but this isn't true. I watched a YouTube clip online. Ever since I was little, Dad made sure TV was "a privilege." In other words, a toy just for him. If he caught me touching the remote at the motel, I was in big trouble.

"Why didn't you call that number and turn yourself in?"

He doesn't get it.

Dad's got me trained. Keep your mouth shut. Don't trust anybody. The world's out to get you. Does this guy really think I'm going to talk to the police? Hey, it's me. The girl who's been missing for ten years.

"I'm not talking to cops."

"You think the police are going to lock you up? Is that it?"

Not me. Dad.

"Okay." Kareem crosses his arms. "I'm not buying it. If you're my wife's daughter, what makes you so scared to turn yourself in?"

It's not the cops. For real. I've lied straight to their faces so many times, I've lost count. When they caught me breaking into some dude's Honda last summer, I told them it was my brother's car. And they actually believed it. Talk about stupid. Not as stupid as the driver. He left his wallet on the front seat (It's super easy to pop the window on an old-school Honda, by the way. Especially if you've got a screwdriver).

No, the cops don't scare me. It's the blank space between now and what happens next. Yeah, that scares me more than any jail I can imagine. And, believe me, I'm pretty good at imagining the worst.

"I don't want my dad to get hurt."

Kareem smirks. "You expect me to believe that?"

Now I'm getting pissed. What's this guy's deal anyway? I don't expect Kareem to understand where I'm coming from. Those freaking Nikes look like they cost a lot. I bet he never had to worry about his dad getting locked up.

"Listen," he says. "That excuse doesn't fly with me."

"It's not an excuse."

"If you're really trying to find your mother, there must be a reason you've been quiet so long."

I glance up at the tree. There's a nail glinting in the trunk, along with the clawed foot of a bird. Somebody tacked it to the skin of that tree like a silent wish. They trusted in something they couldn't see. Why can't I do that?

"If Dad goes to jail…" I can't even say it out loud. "He's not a bad person. If he gets locked up, he'll probably kill himself."

Kareem doesn't look convinced. "After what he did? This is how you feel about that man?"

Dad's put me through hell. No joke. Still, he always watched over me. At the truck stops between cities, he'd stand outside the van with a flashlight in one hand and a can of mace in the other.

"You don't know shit about my dad."

"True, true," Kareem says. "But here's what I don't understand. Why didn't you just run away?"

He makes it sound so easy. Yeah, I thought about it. Lots of times. Dad told me Mom was dead. If I ran away, the cops would lock me up in juvie. He said I'd starve on the streets without him. And, of course, I believed it.

Kareem shakes his head. "Is it money? That's what you want?"

"I want to see my mom."

"That's what you keep saying. Well, I'm not buying this thing you've got going, miss."

"Please let me talk to her."

"Without the police, you mean?"

"If you call the cops, it's over."

"You keep saying that you want to protect your dad. If you ask me, it sounds like you're trying to protect yourself."

What's that supposed to mean? Protect myself? As long as I can remember, my life has revolved around Dad. Who says my mom's going to want me? She's got her own life now. And I'm not a little kid anymore. Maybe she'd dump me in some fucked-up foster home. I mean, seriously. Who knows how she's going to handle it? Her daughter, back from the dead.

Kareem balls up my Communion dress and shoves it in his backpack. I want to scream at him. Give back what's mine. Instead, I lean closer to the ceiba tree. Above me, the branches sway, keeping time with traffic.

"Please," I say again. "Just tell my mom I'm okay."

"Are you?"

I stare at the coins in the dirt.

It's not about Dad anymore.

It's about me.

When I lift my head, Kareem's digging in his pocket. He holds out a phone and I swallow hard. Is he going to call the cops?

"You can tell her yourself," he says quietly.

I can't let it happen this way. Yeah, I want to talk to my mom. God, I want that more than anything.

"It has to be my way."

"Fine." The phone glows in his fist.

"Does she check her messages online? Or do you delete everything before she has a chance to see it?"

"I can make an exception."

"Will she write back?"

"That depends."

"On what?"

Kareem shoves the phone in his pocket. "If she believes you."

At this moment, that's all I can hope for.

"Are you going to leave now?" I ask.

"You're the boss," he says, backing away.

He turns and starts heading toward the street lights. I watch until finally he's gone. I need to get out of here. Fast. He could be on his phone right now, calling the cops.

I take off running past houses with burnt-looking trees on their front lawns. Most of the windows are Xed out with masking tape. Dad says it won't stop glass from breaking in a hurricane. He's always going off about stupid ideas and the brainless morons who believe in them.

When I reach the end of the block, I glance back at the tree, as if it might drag me underground.

I'll take my chances.

20

The train rattles above the highway, lurching from one station to the next. I lean back against the hard plastic seat. The best thing about the Mover? A ride costs absolutely nothing. Can't beat that price. Right now, I'm just going in circles, trying to stay awake. If I fall asleep, a lot of bad things could happen.

Now I'm finally on my own, but it doesn't feel so great. I'm hiding in the back of the train. A bunch of homeless-looking dudes just got on at the last stop. Technically, I'm homeless too, but like I said, it's different for girls. You're always waiting for somebody to steal something from you.

The dudes take turns, passing around a crumpled bag. They tip back their heads, chugging deep as the robo-voice on this driverless train tells us to please stand clear of the door and hold the handrails. Yeah, that's the least of my problems.

Transfer here for...Metrorail...and...Third Street Station, the robo-voice stutters, like it can't make up its mind.

Looking down at the highway, all the traffic is speeding north. The same fancy cars that zoom past the motel at night, headed to the beach or wherever rich people go on vacation. Not here. That's for sure.

My brain is going in circles too. I think about that guy at the motel, the way he put his hands on me, as if I was his property. He wanted to hurt me. Take something for free. Something that didn't belong to him.

I think about me and Shawn holding hands before we jumped. My hair still smells like that water, tangled with salt.

I think about my mom's name.

I think about a lot of things.

On the other side of the train, the dudes bust out laughing for no reason. Or maybe I'm the reason. They keep looking over here, sizing me up. I squeeze against the window, trying to make myself invisible. Right. That always works.

I really need to sleep.

Can't fall asleep on the train. It's too risky. I'll have to find a safe place to crash for the night. But where?

The window's all scratched up with graffiti. It's a secret language, one voice calling to the next. I squint through the bleary glass at a construction site rising above the street. Behind it is the water, but you'd never know. There's only the jumble of metal and concrete. Big-ass hotels. Apartments that look like big-ass hotels. I can't even see the beach from here, the mangrove trees, their roots that tiptoe above land.

An empty Coke can rolls against my foot. I glance up, startled. These dudes are super-sketchy, but they don't seem interested in me. Their primary concern is getting wasted. At least, that's what I'm thinking until this guy with a shaved head plops down next to me.

"Here." Baldie shoves the paper bag in my lap.

I'm so freaked out, I can't move. I just sit there, trying to pretend this isn't happening. The bag's stapled shut, the creases spattered with grease. On the other side of the train, the dudes laugh and clap like it's all a big joke.

I'm the joke.

Baldie and his crew get off at the next stop. Government Center. Where are they going? A homeless convention? When they're finally gone, I rip open the bag. Inside is a Styrofoam take-out box. What the hell? There's a half-eaten hamburger and a handful of withered fries. I'm so hungry, I don't give a shit. I just dive right in. Bon appétit.

No steak ever tasted this good. Not that I've eaten a lot of steaks. When I'm done stuffing my face, it hits me. That dude must've thought I was homeless. Can you blame him? I can't imagine how disgusting I look right now. The duct tape covering the holes in my jeans probably has holes.

The Mover rolls around a couple more times. I can't pass out here and my stomach's about to explode. Maybe that dude laced the burger with cyanide. Great. If I'm going to live like a sky rat, I might as well die like one.

God, I'm starting to lose it.

I stumble off the train and head for the stairs. This place is so freaking huge, I don't know where I'm going. Nobody's on the platform. Just a bench splattered with bird poop and behind it, a sign that says TO STREET.

As I clomp down the steps, a siren cuts through the eerie silence. Instinctively, I press against the concrete wall. I don't want Dad to go to jail. And I sure as hell don't want to go to juvie. Or some fucked-up foster home. I need to figure this out for myself.

I have my mom's name.

That's more than I ever had.

The house at the construction site is empty. It's more like a house-in-progress. Concrete blocks stacked into walls. A blue tarp flapping over the roof. Windows boarded up with plywood, like it's getting ready for a zombie apocalypse.

I learned how to pick a lock when I was a little kid. Dad taught me that trick. I pull the clip out of my hair—a metal barrette shaped like a butterfly. Then I shove it in the doorknob and wiggle it around. Nothing else to it. When I hear the magic click, I turn the knob.

Thanks, Dad.

I dig inside my bag and find my trusty super lighter. Flick it once, twice. I half-expect to see a hobo camp or something. Maybe another kid like me, looking for a place to have sex or get high. Instead, I see a massive refrigerator. Stainless steel. Probably never been used.

God, this is really creeping me out. I'd almost say this place is haunted, but I can't because nobody ever lived here.

One time, me and Dad camped out in a mansion. That's what he called that rotten old house. A mansion. Don't ask where. Maybe on the Georgia line. I have no freaking clue. I was too little to understand why we were "camping" indoors.

I bet that mansion was amazing back in the day. The wooden floors creaked under my feet as if whispering a secret. It even had a grand piano. All the keys were chipped like broken teeth. When I touched it, Dad smacked my hand.

"You want the bad guys to find us?"

We rolled our sleeping bags on the floor. Dad said we were safe from the coyotes that roamed the woods at night, but it wasn't the wild animals that scared me. The living room was filled with broken stuff. Chairs with missing arms. A hole in the ceiling where a chandelier used to be.

"Somebody took off with it. Probably made a ton of money. Now there's nothing worth taking." Dad shook his head like he was disappointed.

It was so cold in that house, we could see our breath steaming. All night, it rained. I listened as water splatted from the ceiling. It puddled on the floor where we slept. Or tried to sleep. I kept my eyes wide open, watching for ghosts. There were paintings nailed to the wall—men with thick mustaches and funny hats.

Maybe they were bad guys too.

Dad never took anything from those shattered places. I bet he would've torn that room to shreds if we found anything he could steal. He wasn't very good at it. Stealing, I mean. That was my job.

After a quick inspection—all empty rooms—I stretch out on the kitchen floor, surrounded by gleaming appliances. Well, at least it's clean. I've definitely slept in worse places. I tug off my bandana and lay it flat on the ground. It's my pillow tonight.

A shout cuts through the dark. Somebody's outside. I scan the room for a hiding spot. There's just blank space. I'm trapped unless I can squeeze inside that fancy refrigerator. My heart's thudding so hard, it might bust through my ribs.

"Stop," a girl calls out, but she's laughing, as if she's just having fun with her friends.

After a while, the voices drift away and I remember how

to breathe. I curl up in a ball like I used to do, back when I believed in ghosts. Then I sink into the long, sweat-drenched gloom of sleep.

అం

There's no sunrise. Only a faint shift of light behind the boarded-up windows. My legs are sticky with dirt and sweat. It's hot as hell inside this empty house. Maybe I am in hell. Or a hole deep in the center of the earth like Shawn told me, the day I laughed at the sparks in the palm of his hand.

It's morning and I'm already sweating. At least I made it through the night without getting jumped, mugged, or attacked by face-eating zombies. Got to celebrate the small stuff.

One time, just before school got out last summer, it was too hot to sleep in the van, so me and Dad slept in a park. We spread our sleeping bags on the playground, right under the plastic slide. The next morning, I was surrounded by dozens of quarters glinting in the sun.

"That's why I keep you around," Dad told me.

He wasn't kidding.

A couple days later, I woke up and got my period for the first time. I was too embarrassed to tell Dad, so I just wadded up a bunch of toilet paper and dealt with it until I got to school. I asked this random girl in homeroom, Tara Frasier, for a tampon. I was probably the only girl in ninth grade who hadn't gotten it yet.

Alone in the bathroom stall, I gawked at the little plastic thing in my hand. I understood the basic concept. Not the exact details. Sometimes you have to figure stuff out for yourself.

Footsteps thud across the ceiling. The construction workers. They must be on the roof. How can I get out of here without them seeing me? There's no place to go. I have to leave the way I came.

Slowly, I unlock the door and step outside. There's a tall, bearded man standing in the front yard. He's wearing a plastic hard hat and a sweat-stained tank top. And he's looking at me.

"Where did you come from?" he asks, blinking.

"I needed a place to sleep."

"Well, you can't sleep here." The guy softens a little. Maybe he thinks I'm a runaway. My mom and dad kicked me out of the house.

"Please," I tell him. "Just let me go."

The man studies my face. "I saw you on TV," he says, moving closer. "You're that girl. The one who's been missing for years."

He sees me.

I slam past the guy and take off running across the empty lot. I've got a head start, but he's already gaining on me. By the time I reach the chain-link fence, my lungs are on fire. I drop to my hands and knees like a kid and start crawling.

I'm under the fence when a hand clamps down on my boot. I try to shake him off, but his grip is locked around my ankle.

"Let go," I scream at him.

All it takes is one good tug. The boot falls off.

Goodbye Super Glue shoe.

I'm sort of half-limping, half-stumbling toward the Mover station. It's different here in the daylight. Moms with strollers. An old man in a suit gulping a fancy coffee, the kind that's mostly foam. A group of elementary school kids in matching purple T-shirts bolt upstairs, swinging their backpacks like weapons.

"Okay, troops," says a tired-looking woman near the Mover entrance. "Let's stick together." She's got a clipboard in her hand. Dark sunglasses. A ponytail tucked under a baseball cap. This must be their teacher.

The kids get in line and file into the Mover. I tag along, hoping nobody pays attention to me. The train lurches forward and I lean against the scratched-up window, keeping my head down. Beside me, a little girl in braids sits by herself. God, I remember being that girl. Always new and out of place.

"Leigh," the teacher calls out, "what did I say about sticking together?"

The girl scoots off the seat and goes over to the others.

If we don't stick together, the bad guys will find us.

Is that little girl still hidden inside me? Or have I changed? I'm no longer the girl who listened to the trees as her hair floated in the stream.

I'm somebody else.

ॐ

The Mover stops in front of the library downtown. I follow the kids as if I belong on this field trip. They're a lot younger than me, but it's safer to move in a group, if you don't want to attract attention.

As we march toward the library, we pass a man sleeping on the sidewalk. These kids are acting like they've never seen a homeless person before. The boys laugh and crack jokes about dead bodies.

"Settle down," their teacher says, chopping the air like a drill sergeant. "Nothing to get excited about." No big deal. Just another homeless guy passed out on a sheet of cardboard.

Libraries have always been my safe place. I can't believe how nice it is here. Almost as nice as the Bryant's fancy house with the glass walls. If only I could hang out and read all day. This time I'm not here for the books.

I watch the teacher lead her class inside the building. In a way, it feels like I never got to be a kid. I never went to camp. Never tried out for soccer or band. All that shit costs money. And money's one thing we never had.

As I head inside, the concrete slaps against the bottom of my left heel. I'll have to deal with that later. I should toss my other boot in the trash, but going without shoes is never a good idea. Especially if I need to run.

The library has that dirt-free, air-conditioned smell that I don't get to enjoy very often (unless I'm at school, which isn't enjoyable on any level). It's so damn clean, I'm scared to touch anything. Even the books look like decorations.

Heads turn as I dip past the shelves. That's when I start to get nervous. Did these people see my face on TV? The little girl and her dad reading *Frog and Toad*. The boy with a pierced lip exactly like mine.

Do they see me?

I sit down at the farthest desk in the back. This computer is ancient and takes forever to wake up. Finally, the welcome screen begins to glow. I get online and click over to Facebook.

NEW MESSAGE:

If you are my daughter,
give me proof.

She wrote back.

It's not the message I was hoping for, but my mom wrote back to me. At first, I'm all excited, right? Then I read it again and my heart sinks. Mom sounds kind of pissed. Kareem said she gets a ton of messages from people all over the world pretending to be me. Yeah, I'd be pissed too.

I stare at her message. It's like she's shouting at me and I don't know what to do. How can I prove I'm for real? I try to remember the yellow house where I used to live. It was so long ago, it's like holding onto a dream.

I had a swing in my backyard...

No, that's not going to work. Anybody can see the swing in that picture from the newspaper. Why can't I remember something about Mom? She's on the other side of the computer screen. What can I say to make her believe me? All I have are Dad's stories. In other words, his lies. But there's something in the space between here and now. The words he left out. That's where I find the answer.

You and Dad swam with the jellyfish.

❧

"How's it going over here?"

I glance up.

I've been sitting at this computer for hours, waiting for Mom to write back. Her message was sent this morning, Saturday. How often does she look at her Facebook page? Maybe she only checks it after work. I mean, she's got to have a normal job?

"Just letting you know we're closing soon," the guy says, thumping my desk. He's got a button that says, *I'm a librarian. What's your superpower?* and a sweet pair of checkered socks. Please don't look at me.

The cool librarian crouches next to my desk. "We've got pizza, if you're hungry. The Anime Club's watching *Spirited Away.* We've seen it a million times, but who cares?"

Pizza sounds good right now. More than good. I haven't eaten anything all day. Still, I don't turn around.

"You're not a vegetarian, are you?" he asks, wiping his glasses on his shirt. "Our club president, Daniella? She doesn't eat anything with a face. And I'm like, yeah? Well, pizza doesn't have a face."

"I'll eat anything," I tell him.

He gives me a thumbs-up.

I follow him around the corner into the auditorium. It's dark in here, but I'm still terrified that someone will recognize me. Everybody's hanging around a big table, munching on pizza. A couple of girls smile when I reach for a slice. Maybe they think I'm friend-worthy.

I want that so bad.

When the movie's over, I'm the only person left with nowhere to go. For some reason, there's just one boy. He's got a clump of rubber bracelets on his wrist and greasy-looking hair combed over his face.

"Did you like it?" he mumbles.

"What?" I stare at a smashed-up piece of gum on the floor.

"The best part is when No-Face starts puking."

He's talking about the movie.

"Yeah. Um. That was great."

Actually, it was kind of great.

"See you next week," he says, taking off.

Another boy is walking toward us, waving his phone like a torch. Probably the kid's older brother. They have the same sloped walk, their blue-jeaned legs moving in sync. I watch them disappear. Then I'm alone again.

After he's gone, I head back to the computers. The library's closing any minute. Half the lights are turned off and I can barely see where I'm going. I stumble through the rows of chairs. If I turn on a computer, I'll give myself away. Not that I have a choice. I push the power button and the screen lights up.

"Unbelievable."

It's my new friend, the cool librarian.

"We're closing," he says, as if I forgot.

I try to come up with an excuse, but I can tell he's not going to listen. "I just need to send a message."

"You can talk to your boyfriend later," he says.

I think about Shawn and all the stuff that happened last night. I'll be lucky if he ever talks to me again.

"It won't take long."

He sighs. "You've been on that computer for hours."

It's pretty obvious he wants to go home.

"Just one more minute."

"The library's closed."

"Please? I just need to tell my mom I'm here."

He looks at me.

"One minute," he says, walking away.

I've got sixty seconds.

Mom still hasn't written back. At that point, I'm beginning to think she never will. There's nothing I can do to make her believe me.

Meanwhile, the librarian is walking around the desks, shutting off computers. I want to tell him that he's my hero. Instead, I hunch lower in my seat. Maybe he'll lock me up inside the library, just like this book I read when I was little.

"Can you shut down that computer for me?" he asks.

Yeah, I can shut it down.

Or not.

When I do a search for Shawn on Facebook, nothing comes up, but that doesn't mean he's not online. I remember him joking about his graphic novel. *I'm Mostly Okay*. Maybe it wasn't a joke after all.

There's one thing I haven't tried yet. I've got a secret Twitter that's sadly been neglected. It's mostly *Doctor Who* stuff and random GIFs I've retweeted.

I type his name into Twitter and his profile pops up right away. Guess there aren't a lot of Shawn Bryants in the Twitterverse. And he's got thousands of fans. God, I had no idea he was so popular online. It's like he's the star of his own secret world.

Every tweet is swarming with cartoons. Did he make all these drawings by himself? I scroll through doodles of people I recognize from school. There's Ms. Vitelli in the front office, breathing fire like a dragon. The baseball team getting stomped by Optimus Prime. The toothy faces have captions like, *How dare you insult me!* It's freaking hilarious, of course. So this is the graphic novel he told me about.

When I reach the last drawing on his page, I suck in a breath. It's a pencil sketch of a house on stilts. In the distance, a chain of dolphins leap through the waves, and a girl steers a boat into a flash of green.

Shawn drew a picture of me.

In his drawing, I actually look sort of pretty. He even drew the Stain on my face, but for some reason, I don't mind. At the top of the screen, there's a box that says, FOLLOW.

So I do.

Then I send a message:

> Shawn,
>
> You're a really amazing artist. Why didn't you tell me before? I want to start getting to know you better. If you never talk to me again, I'll understand. I'm sorry I let you down. My life is out of control right now (I guess that's kind of obvious).
>
> I can't stop thinking about our boat ride to Stiltsville.

When you kissed me, it felt so amazing. I didn't want it to end.

I hope we still have a chance.

SNAKE BITE < 3

I'm about to push back my chair, then I remember that I forgot to sign out of Facebook. When I click on it, there's a note at the top of the page:

Where can we meet?

I stare at the words on the computer screen.

My mom wrote back.

Does this mean she believes I'm her daughter?

I rack my brains, trying to think of a safe place to meet. Starbucks. That's only a block away. I walked past it this morning.

I type: STARBUCKS ON FLAGLER.

Then I add, NO POLICE.

The librarian leans over my shoulder and punches a button on the computer. The screen goes dark. I have no clue if my message got through in time. I didn't tell Mom when to meet. What the hell is wrong with me? I mean, seriously. How could I be so stupid? I slump back in my seat.

"You're not in some kind of trouble, are you?" the librarian wants to know. He's sizing me up. Trying to figure out where he's seen my face. My Stain. "We're closed now. Do you have somewhere to go?"

"Yeah," I tell him. "My mom's waiting for me."

"Is she on her way?"

I nod. "She's going to be here soon."

"Glad to hear it. Can I walk you out?"

Together we walk past the shelves of magazines and books. He pushes the door open for me and we step outside. It's getting dark now and it's starting to rain. Not a full-on downpour. More like the sky is squeezed out and dripping all it's got left.

I have no idea where to go.

The librarian takes out an umbrella. "Good luck. I hope you don't wait long," he says, snapping it open.

As he heads for the stairs, I watch him walk away.

"Thank you," I whisper, though I know he can't hear me.

21

When the rain finally slows to a drizzle, I head out into the street. Downtown is all parking lots and big-ass hotels. The only green things are palm trees held up by wobbly planks, as if they're too weak to stand on their own. As I start walking to the coffee shop, there's a lot on my mind.

Is Mom going to show up? Or will she flake out on me? And what am I supposed to say to her? I haven't seen my mom since I was a little kid. Yeah, we're biologically connected, but that doesn't mean we're going to be besties.

All my life, Dad's been my world. It's always been me and him. Now I'm on my own for the first time. I'm not sure how I feel about that. It's scary, but exciting too. I've wanted it for so long. The chance to be free.

I think about the drawings Shawn posted on Twitter. His graphic novel was so funny and amazing. Not to mention, smart. A trifecta of awesome. He's a really talented artist, but at school, he's always so quiet. Guess I'm not the only one with a secret. I just hope he gives me a second chance.

Will I ever see him again?

When I reach Starbucks, the tables are packed. Business dudes. A bunch of moms with those over-the-shoulder baby slings that remind me of cocoons. I can't find a place to sit down, so I hang out near the counter.

"Are you going to order?" asks the guy behind the cash register. Barista. Whatever he's called.

I stare at the menu on the wall. Mocha frappucino. Caramel brulée latte. I can't even pronounce half this stuff.

"Can I just have a plain coffee?"

"House blend?" he says, like it's really complicated. "What size?"

"Small, I guess."

"You mean tall?"

"Sure."

"Room for milk?"

"Okay." Why is this so hard?

"Name?"

I'm tempted to give him a fake name. Something dumb like when you've got a sub in homeroom and they're taking attendance. Princess Elsa. Bella Swan.

"Reece," I tell him.

"With two Es?"

Now he's making fun of me. "Three, actually."

"Got it."

He scurries behind the counter. I try to focus on the jangly music blasting overhead. I'm so nervous, I keep glancing at the door every five seconds. It feels like everybody's watching me, but they're so into their caffeine fix, they don't notice I'm alive. No wonder Dad says the safest place to hide is in a crowd.

The barista dude clunks a steaming paper cup on the counter. He doesn't ask for money, which is a good thing because I don't have any. I'm thinking he's made a mistake. Then I spot REECE scribbled across the lid and below my name, a star.

"On the house," he says.

I smile. "Thanks."

Dad says that bad guys rule the world. Everybody's out to get you. Well, he's wrong. Sure, there's plenty of bad people, but that doesn't mean I should expect the worst all the time.

Now that I've claimed my table, I can use the facilities. When I say *use*, I mean it's bird bath time. I leave my cup on a table and head for the restroom. It's locked, of course, so I have to wait.

A minute later, the door swings open and a woman rushes out. She's got the whole jeans-and-heels thing going on and she smells really nice. Can't say the same for myself. As if this

wasn't beyond embarrassing, she makes a big deal about scooting out of my way.

"Excuse me," she says, mopping her face with a napkin.

Maybe she's got her own problems.

Coffee shop restrooms are always hit or miss. This one gets a
high score because it's just a single stall. Points off for the auto-
matic hand dryer. They've got one of those industrial-strength
air blowers. I really hate when there's no paper towels. I always
save a handful, just in case.

Somebody's pounding on the door, but they can take a
number. When I'm done splashing at the sink, I check myself
out. Not bad for a girl who spent the night at a construction
site. Not great, either. My boot's about to fall off and my jeans
are hanging by a duct-taped thread. The T-shirt's okay, I guess.
Black's always been my favorite non-color.

All of a sudden, I'm so freaking scared.

Can I just stay here forever?

What if Mom sees me and she's like, *Wait. On second thought,
no thanks.* Or what if she doesn't believe I'm for real? Only one
way to find out. As much as I want to run and hide, that's Dad's
style. Not mine.

I head over to wobbly table. Still no sign of Mom. I'm starting to think she isn't going to show up. What if she changed
her mind? I sit back and gulp my free coffee. The cup's almost
empty.

I've got to make it last.

Hours later, my coffee's long gone and Mom still hasn't shown
up. It's pretty obvious she's not coming. I dump my cup in the
trash and head outside into the cool early evening air.

All the tables on the sidewalk are taken. Great. I squat down
on the pavement with my back against the wall. My hands shake
as I reach for my pack of menthols, but there aren't any left.

I watch a dark-haired woman in a lacy blouse tap a cigarette
out of the carton. I can't help noticing that she's all alone. She

takes a drag, then stares out at the street, like the secrets of the universe are hidden in the push-pull of traffic.

It's the woman I saw in the bathroom, the one who was crying. God, we walked right past each other. She glances up and says my name.

My real name.

At first, I'm too scared to move. Then she reaches out and pulls me into a hug. It feels so strange, letting her get close. I lean into her arms. I've wanted this for so long. My mom holding me.

"Look at you." She keeps looking at my face. I mean, really looking.

Slowly, I pull away.

She does this thing, touching my hair, then her own. "I'm here now," Mom says, like she's the one who's been missing.

I'm kind of giving her a hard time. What the hell am I supposed to do? She hasn't been in my life for almost a decade. And my mom is so fancy. I didn't expect that. It makes me feel even grungier, standing next to her.

This is really awkward.

Without thinking, I reach into the ashtray on her table and swipe a cigarette. The tip is smudged with glossy pink lipstick. I'm not a big fan of pink. Or lipstick. Still, I breathe in the smoke.

Mom snatches it out of my hand. She flicks it on the ground, scattering a trail of sparks. "Want to get cancer?" she says, all judgey.

Yeah, we're off to a great start.

I used to imagine what it would be like, getting back together with Mom. When me and Dad were sleeping in the van, I'd stare at the power lines in the windshield and pretend they were strong enough to hold me. If I could sprint across those wires, they'd carry me back to the mango tree. And then I'd be home.

Mom glances at the other tables. God, what if somebody recognizes us? What if they hold up their phones and take a picture? Remember that girl who was abducted a long time ago? I just took a selfie with her!

"Your father's not around, is he?" Mom asks, reading my mind.

"No," I tell her. "I came by myself."

"That was brave."

Brave?

Nobody's ever called me that before.

"Want to take a walk?" she asks.

I do.

Mom grabs her purse and starts clip-clopping down West Flagler in her strappy heels. I follow behind like we aren't even together. Mom stays quiet at first. Next thing I know, she's blabbing nonstop.

"You're so grown up," she says.

I shrug. "It happens."

"But you're still a tiny thing," she adds, looking at me again. "Remember you used to climb that tree?"

"The mango tree?"

"Yes. And I'd call you my little monkey."

I don't remember.

She stares at my feet. "What happened to your shoe?"

When we walk past the construction site, I glance back at that empty house where I slept on the concrete. There's a mango tree in the front yard. Why didn't I notice before? Guess I was too busy trying not to get jumped.

Another thing I didn't notice. If I had kept going a couple blocks, I would've reached the water. It was there all along. I just didn't walk far enough. The Miami River sparkles under the street lights. Boats tilt and sway, their ropes clanging like wind chimes in the breeze.

"I never stopped looking for you," Mom says, wiping her eyes. "Everybody told me not to give up hope. The police said you were gone. They told me it would be better if I just let go."

She covers her face with her hand, sobbing in little hiccups. My mom's super pretty, even when she's blowing snot out of her nose. When I cry, my cheeks get all splotchy and I look like a blowfish.

That's when I notice the ring.

It's not like I expected my mom to stay single. Let's be real. She's not getting back together with Dad anytime soon. I mean, this isn't some Disney princess movie. But it definitely feels weird, seeing that gold ring looped around her finger.

Mom catches my stare. "Kareem and I got married last year. Same house, though," she says, smiling.

Before I can say anything, Mom reaches into her purse and takes out her phone. She swipes her thumb across the screen and clicks through photo after photo.

"You're really into taking pictures, huh?"

"It's so easy with this phone," she says, swiping away. "Kareem showed me how."

I peek over her shoulder at the phone. My mom takes pictures of the most random crap. An airplane wing slicing through clouds. The speckled nose of a puppy squished between somebody's knees.

"That's Lalo," she says. "He can't sleep unless we turn on The Weather Channel. Guess he takes after me."

When I was little, I really wanted a puppy. Dad always told me no. He said we couldn't afford a dog and besides, he had allergies. I'm supposed to be allergic too. How would I know? I've never held a dog in my whole life.

"It's here somewhere." Mom flicks past a close-up of scrambled eggs heaped on a plate. Why do people take pictures of their breakfast? Maybe so they can remember what they ate. Actually, Mom's pictures are kind of cool. She makes even the most boring things seem amazing.

"You're good at this."

Mom shakes her head. "It's just for fun."

"No, I mean it."

She's showing me her world, but when I look at her pictures, it's like studying a distant planet through a telescope.

"Found it," she says, passing the phone to me.

The yellow house. It's exactly the same. My swing in the front yard. The rope bleeding into the tree bark. I try to zoom in closer. The screen changes to a different picture—a little girl digging in the sand on the beach. She's got a halo of curls and a determined look on her face.

"Who's this?" I ask.

Mom doesn't say anything. After a minute, she says, "That's your sister Gabriela."

I stare at that picture for a long time.

Ever since I can remember, I've wanted a big sister.

Now that's what I am.

"She reminds me of you," Mom says. "I mean, when you were that age. A big ball of energy. Never slows down."

"How old is she?"

"Gaby just turned three."

My little sister's been on the planet for three years. And I didn't even know she existed until now.

"Can I meet her?"

"Of course." Mom squeezes my hand.

There's something a little off in her smile. She's got this whole new life without me. Does she really need me in it?

"I want you to understand," she says, looking right at me. "I never stopped believing you'd come home. Every year, I'd light a candle on your birthday and make a wish." She smiles again, but it quickly fades. "When your father took you away, he took a piece of me too."

"Why did he do it?"

It's a question I've been carrying inside forever. There's no right answer. I just need to hear for myself.

"He wanted to hurt me," she says. "And he did."

I don't know what to believe anymore. My mom is so different from what I expected. She's nothing like what Dad told me. Or maybe she's changed. Can you keep changing after you've grown up?

I hand her back the phone. As she reaches for it, her sleeve hikes up, and that's when I see it. The scar. A rusty chain swirling across her skin.

"We were just kids when we were on the road," she explains. "Not much older than you, actually. Your dad was in a lot of trouble."

"What kind of trouble?"

"You know. Snatch-and-grab." Mom searches for the words. "We were staying at this RV park. He stole a lot of money."

All this time, I've been stealing for Dad.

I didn't think he was any good at it.

He was the biggest thief of all.

Mom watches the boats drift across the water. "I'm sure your father's told you a lot of things."

"He told me you were dead."

"Well, obviously, that's not true."

"He said the bad guys were after us." I'm rambling now. It's all coming out, everything I've held inside. "That night we left, I saw you lying on the floor."

"We had some pretty bad fights," she says, shaking her head. "Your father couldn't find work. He was drinking too much. Things got pretty bad. My cousin tried to help him get a job down in Homestead. Tomato-picking. But it didn't pay enough."

"Wait." I'm trying to process what she just said. "I have family here?"

She nods. "Cousins. Uncles. Aunts too."

"He never told me."

"They're here in Miami. You can meet them when you're ready."

It's almost too much to take in. I'm used to the idea of being alone. Dad cut me off from my entire family.

He stole my life.

"Dad said you didn't want me."

It just slips out.

"And you believed him," she says quietly.

What was I supposed to think?

Mom hugs me so close, it squeezes all the breath out of me. For a while, we just stay like that, holding each other. When she finally pulls away, her eyes are wet. "I didn't plan on having kids so young. But that doesn't mean I didn't want you."

"Really?" I'm blinking away tears.

"I've wanted you since the moment I held you in my arms," she says, hugging me tighter. "And I want you to come and stay with us."

When she says this, I fly out of my skin and soar over those fancy boats on the water. My mom wants me, no matter what Dad said. It was his biggest lie of all. That's what makes it so much harder—the words I'm about to say.

"I need to go back first."

"Go back where?"

I can hear the panic in her voice.

"Back to see my dad."

She shakes her head. "I've already lost you once."

"He can't hurt me anymore."

When I say it out loud, I know it's true.

"Please don't do this." Mom's begging me not to leave. She doesn't understand why I need to go back to that motel.

I'm giving my dad something he never gave me.

The chance to say goodbye.

22

It's dark by the time we park across from the motel. From the curb, it looks like a place you might want to visit. The Surfside's neon sign glows above the street. I can't see what's hidden beneath the glare. An empty swimming pool. Rooms that smell like bleach and cigarettes. A little girl huddled on the stairs, clutching her naked doll.

"So this was your home." Mom grips the steering wheel.

The Surfside was never anybody's home. I feel sick, just looking at that neon sign and all its promises. "Yeah, this is it."

"You don't have to go inside," she says.

I swear my mom has psychic powers.

"I can handle it."

She looks at me for a long time. "I'm sure you can."

When she squeezes my hand, I squeeze back.

"This is going to be quick, okay?" Why am I whispering? It's not like Dad can hear me.

"You're not going alone," she says.

"If Dad sees you, he's going to freak out."

"Let him."

Together we get out of the car.

As we cross the street, I'm on high alert. Every little noise sets me off. I know all these sounds by heart. The palm fronds rustling above the parked cars. The ACs rattling in their cages. The dull hum of a motel room where nobody talks at all.

Last summer, I used to watch the little girl scoop up bottle caps. It already feels like forever ago. What did she hope to find buried in the dirt? A glimpse of something shiny and perfect? Or a tiny piece of the Surfside that she could hold in her fist, sharp edges and all?

The lights are on in the motel room. My old room. Except

it wasn't really mine. For a second, I think about walking back to the car. It would be so easy. All I have to do is turn around.

I can't stop thinking about Dad. What the hell am I going to say? He stole everything from me. All that makes me who I am. Still, he was always there, keeping me safe. I think about those nights he stood outside the van with a flashlight and a can of mace, looking for the bad guys.

Somebody's in the parking lot. More than one somebody. The voices float toward me, but I can't make out the words.

Booth.

Who's he talking to? Maybe someone's moving in. People come and go so fast around here, it's hard to keep up.

I wait at the bottom of the stairs, listening hard. There's a man walking across the parking lot with Booth. Dark jeans. White T-shirt. No creases, as if he just ripped it out of the package. This guy isn't a sky rat. He's way too clean.

"The rooms are all the same?" he asks.

"That's right," Booth says. "Except for who's in them."

As he moves past the street lamp, I catch a glimpse of his lean face. The cop I saw at school.

He's here.

Mom looks at me. Before she has a chance to move, I bolt up the stairs. My legs burn as I pound the steps. When I reach the motel door, I knock, but there's no answer. I twist the knob back and forth, trying to bust it open. Then I glance back at the breezeway and there's Mouse, sitting on the steps.

"What's wrong?" she asks, combing the doll's hair with her fingers.

"Police," I tell her.

Mouse's dark brown eyes get even bigger. She motions for me to come inside her room and I shake my head. Yeah, I could sneak in there and hide. But I'm done with hiding.

"Can you keep a secret?" I whisper.

"Yeah," she says. "I'm real good at keeping secrets."

"Don't say anything, okay? Just go back inside. And don't come out, no matter what you hear."

Mouse blinks. "Okay."

"You promise?"

"Promise."

Slowly, she goes back in her room and closes the door.

I still don't know if her grandmother ratted me out. Right now, I'm thinking that's probably true. No, it has to be true. But it doesn't matter anymore. Booth's going to be here any second. Come on, Dad. Open up. I tap my foot against the cheap plywood.

The door cracks open.

Dad's face hovers above me. "Reece? What the hell are you doing here?"

Well, I'm sort of famous now because my kidnapping—no, my abduction; that's what the guy on TV called it—is all over the news. And I found my mom and she's amazing. And I have a little sister too. And by the way, Dad. You're going to jail.

I shove my way inside.

The room is stripped. I can't believe what I'm seeing. Empty shelves hanging out of the dresser like tongues. Even the carpet is bare. Not a single cardboard box. Dad must've sold every last piece of junk.

"You have to leave," I tell him. "Now."

Code word: T-Rex.

I wait for Dad to freak out. Scream at me. Do something crazy. This is the perfect time for the Ultimate Rage to take effect. Instead, he sinks down on the mattress, cradling his head in his hands.

The door rattles like it's going to explode.

"Open up," Booth yells.

I glance around the motel room, searching for a place to hide, but we're surrounded. No place left. Not even a bed to crawl under. Not even a hole in the center of the earth.

"Okay," Dad says, pacing back and forth. "Okay, okay."

I've never seen him crumble before. I mean, he's scared out of his mind. All of a sudden, I feel so guilty. How stupid is that?

Why am I responsible for all the shit he put me through? Still, I can't stand to see him like this.

I run inside the bathroom. Dad squeezes next to me. I quickly lock the door behind us. The window. It's cracked open. I glance back at Dad. "Can you fit through there?"

"Not a chance," he says, shaking his head. "I'm not skinny like you, needle legs."

"You have to try."

We both squint at the window.

Dad folds his hands together, offering me a boost. "You go first. Go while you have a chance."

"I can't."

Dad's face crumples with hurt. "You're ditching me. Is that it?"

"There's no time. Only one of us can go."

It won't be me.

"We'll move to the beach." Dad's talking real fast. "You don't even have to go to school. What do you say? Doesn't that sound good?"

He's making a deal. Filling my head with lies. Telling me exactly what I want to hear.

Too bad I'm not falling for it.

When I don't move, he lowers his head.

"Please," I say. "Just go."

I look back at the scars lacing his arms.

Swim with the jellyfish.

"Keep your eyes wide open, okay?" Dad kisses my cheek and I know that I'm never going to see him again. "Be brave, needle legs."

Slowly, I turn around.

I don't want him to see my tears.

"Count to a hundred," he tells me.

The numbers float inside my head.

One Mississippi... Two Mississippi.

I turn the doorknob until I hear the lock pop. When I come

out, Booth's standing in the empty motel room with my mom, waiting for me.

"Where's your dad?" he shouts.

I look away.

His new friend, Mr. Plain White Tee, marches into the bathroom, shoving right past me. His gaze tilts up.

The window's pushed open.

Empty.

For a minute, he just stands there, as if Dad's going to soar through that open window like a lost pigeon. Then he turns around. His gaze flicks to my Stain.

"You okay?" he asks.

I nod.

"Can you tell me your name?"

Yeah, I can.

As I step closer, his eyes widen, as if he's seen a ghost. A dead girl brought back to life.

"Christina Stone," he says. "I'd like to ask you some questions."

23

The beach at Key Biscayne is crowded at sunset. As the tide pulls away, I hunt for shells with my little sister.

"Finders keepers," Gaby says, scooping up a conch. She carries the shells to me in her fist. Together we build a castle decorated with the broken pieces. Soon the tide will wash it away, but that doesn't matter. We can build more.

Lalo chases seagulls, yapping as they lift above the sand.

"He takes after me," says Mom, laughing.

"True." Kareem fires up the grill. For days, he's been marinating all kinds of good stuff in the fridge—little plastic bags of mahi mahi, Bahamian fish tacos drizzled with lime. Mom calls him el jefe, the chef.

Shawn stretches next to me on the blanket, sketching the boats that drift near the lighthouse, the zoo cages, empty and abandoned, the floating houses of Stiltsville, dolphins skimming the waves, and all the secret things hidden beneath the tide.

We're still getting used to each other. All of us. It's going to take a while, soaking up my new name. Except it's not really so new. It was there, all along. I just needed to remember.

Mom snaps a picture of us with her phone. "Christina tells me you're an artist," she says, admiring Shawn's sketchbook.

He grins. "Only on my days off."

"And you too." Mom brushes the hair from my eyes. I've let the bleached-out tangles grow long. Even longer than the mermaid hair I dreamed about years ago. "You're my work of art," she whispers.

As the sun melts into the bay, we pass around the paper plates. Shawn's brought grilled corn to share and we eat and eat until there's nothing left. For the first time I can remember, I'm not hungry anymore. I'm full.

"Hold on. I've got a surprise for you," Mom says, opening a box of cupcakes.

We're pretending it's my birthday. Good thing I'm good at pretending. She says it's supposed to make up for all the lost time. Every birthday we've missed. It could never really be the same. Right now, it's close enough.

She plunks a candle on the biggest cupcake. Rainbow sprinkles. My favorite. "We forgot the matches," she says, frowning.

"No worries." Shawn holds out my super lighter. The candle flickers and sparks. It's the tricky kind that supposed to keep you guessing. A light that goes out, then flares over and over like a promise.

"Make a wish," Mom says, but I already know what to do.

I've got a lot of wishes left.

It's been months since Dad slipped through the window to freedom. I try to imagine that he's on another beach across the water, sleeping under stars so bright, you can almost hear them buzzing. Or maybe an island miles away where the jellyfish wash up at dawn.

When my mom holds that candle in front of me, I don't close my eyes. There's no way I'm going to forget this.

I keep my eyes wide open and make a wish.